每周一部電影，增進職場英文力

WATCHING MOVIES TO
LEARN ENGLISH

《利用上班學好英文》娛樂版

從廠商應對、同事相處、出國洽公、外地支援到**商業談判**，

作者從50部電影中
擷取**職場**中可能遇到的**相關用語**，
以及**關鍵用字**，
讓你**說得好**又**說得巧**！

楊偉凱——著

CONTENTS

第1章

如何利用看影片學英文

第2章

你來我往不可少的社交用語

第 3 章

開會談判不可少的關鍵用語

CONTENTS

第 **6** 章

職場中的電話溝通用語

自序
用對方法就能獲得好成效

幾年前我離開台灣的外商銀行，開始在大陸從事諮詢培訓的工作，輔導的對象都是中國人，當然也不可能有接觸英文的機會，語言一旦少接觸必然會生疏，因此，對於無法繼續提升英文能力，心裡感到有點不安。

由於這項新工作的地點是隨著項目而定，至今我的足跡已踏遍中國三分之二的省分了，工作地點也有不少是在二級城市，所以白天工作完後，晚上便沒事幹，然而大陸的電視節目又無法吸引我，所以「看國外電影」變成為我打發時間的主要消遣。

剛開始我把看電影當成純娛樂，偶爾看到一些不錯或沒聽過的英文用法，會稍微留意，但時間久了就很容易忘掉。隨著觀看影片的數量愈來愈多，心想應該把從影片中學到的英文記錄下來，將來有機會可以使用，才不會看完電影後就全忘光了。

於是我開始養成習慣，第一次看還是以娛樂為目的，同時了解全片的內容，但第二遍便是以學習英文為目的，邊看邊記錄一些實用的句子。一段時間後我記錄的影片已有好幾十部了，但說實在的，記錄的句子能脫口而出的還是有限。原因是過程欠缺一個學習的步驟，就是「熟練」，尤其是語言，不練習是不可能熟悉的。

因為考量孩子的教育問題，全家於2015年移居加拿大，到那裡是全英文的環境，所以以前在職場還能夠應付的英文，又變的有點不足了，於是我又有動機想提升英文能力。想到自己過去兩三年整理的英文也不少，而且都是很實用的，我決定在自我學習的同時，也把它寫成書籍，

和讀者分享。

　　但是，撰寫英文書實在是項大工程，加上電影的主題五花八門，涉及的領域又很廣，於是我決定還是延續前兩本書，以職場英語為主，我想這應該也是多數台灣人學英文最迫切的需求。

　　我在外商工作十餘年，加上現在也生活在全英文的環境，很清楚職場中需要用到的實用英文有哪些？所以我重新篩選一些較合適的電影，節錄電影中最實用的英文句子，分門別類整理出職場會使用到的英文，幫助讀者省下寶貴的時間，大家只要把書中的內容熟悉並加以運用，必然能大大提升職場英文的能力。

2016 / 7 / 1 於多倫多

本書結構

①

本書內容主要分為三大部分，第一部分是「情境模擬對話篇」，部分內容是參考電影曾出現的情節，並加以改編成職場實用的情境對話。

情境模擬對話篇

A What have you been up to?
你最近都在忙什麼？

B Nothing much besides work.
除了工作外沒什麼。

A What's up, man?
老兄，你好嗎？

B Terrific.
好極了！

A Everything good?
都好嗎？

---

②

第二部分是「從電影對話中找靈感」，主要是篩選電影中與前述情境相關的台詞或補充職場實用的句子。

從電影對話中找靈感

▶ What have you been doing?
你在忙什麼？ ················· 🎥 安諾瑪麗莎

▶ How have you been getting on?
你近來如何啊？ ················· 🎥 布魯克林

▶ Long time no see.
好久不見。 ················· 🎥 心靈大道

▶ Rough day?
今天很折騰吧！ ················· 🎥 空中救援

▶ It's not my lucky day.
今天運氣不好。 ················· 🎥 空中救援

▶ Are you alright?
你還好嗎？ ················· 🎥 靈犬出任務

---

③

第三部分是「最容易運用的職場關鍵字」，主要是從前述情境中挑出一個職場重要的關鍵單字，說明其如何使用，並以此字衍生出其他片語或單字，同時輔以例句說明其使用情境，以加重本書職場英文的內容。

最容易運用的職場關鍵字　Appreciate

　　當你受到別人的恩惠或幫忙，想表達謝意時，可以用appreciate或thank，但這兩個字有些差異，appreciate的意思是「感激；感謝」，用在你非常了解這件事或物品的價值，就可以說Appreciate it或Much appreciated，感謝的力道比較強，而thank只是對別人的行動或給你好處時禮貌性地回應，比較是一般性的感謝。

　　Appreciate還有另一個意思是指土地、股票或貨幣的價格上升或增值，反義詞是depreciate，就是價格下跌或貶值，兩個字的名詞各為appreciation及depreciation，相關用法請參閱以下例句。

1 Appreciate **V** 感謝；感激
I would appreciate if you can respond to my questions above ASAP.
如果你能盡快回應我上述的問題，我將不勝感激。

2 Appreciated **adj** 感謝的；感激的
Your kind assistance and supports are highly appreciated.
非常感謝你仁慈的協助與支持。

百用句型（進機場大廳）

• Is there _____ near here／around here／nearby?
  這附近有 _____ 嗎？

  ①a pay phone（投幣電話）；
  ②a currency exchange location（換匯的地方）；
  ③any stores selling prepaid cell phone cards（任何商家銷售手機預付卡）；
  ④a 7-Eleven store（7-11便利商店）

④

除了三大主要內容外，為了增加閱讀的趣味性，也隨機加入了不同單元，例如「百用句型」──只要熟悉某個句型，就可以套用不同內容進去。

電影經典名言可以這樣應用

　　這句話可以用在鼓勵別人，有些事情雖然最終結果不如預期，但從過程中仍然可以學到寶貴的經驗。

• **I believe the journey to be more important than the destination.**
我相信過程比目的地更重要。　　　　　　　　　引自《全面進化》

⑤

還有「電影經典名言可以這樣應用」，是篩選電影中曾出現的成語、名言或較發人省思的一段話，以及適合運用的場合或情境。

換種說法也可通

各種不舒服的說法
1	I'm not feeling so well today. 我今天覺得不太舒服。《驚天換日》
2	I feel very achy. 我覺得不舒服。《愛情失控點》
3	Like maybe I'm coming down with something. 可能是我生病了吧！《愛情失控點》
4	It's just a little touch of Delhi／Buddha belly. 只是有點小拉肚子。《聖母峰》
5	My stomach hurts. 我胃疼！《安諾瑪麗莎》
6	I'm actually not feeling so hot. 我真的感覺不舒服。《高年級實習生》

⑥

此外，電影中也常出現和我們平時講法不同的台詞，這些句子將之整理在「換種說法也可通」的單元中，讓讀者學習不同的講法，以豐富自己的英文對話內容。

還有其他單元，便是依照各章節的內容所增，並非所有章節都有，在此不一一臚列，請讀者自行參考各章節內容。

第 1 章

如何利用
看影片學英文

在《利用上班學好英文》一書中曾提及，如果你暫時還沒有機會在有英文環境的公司工作，或是你已經身處英文的工作環境，但由於職位不夠高或負責的工作不常有機會接觸英文，自己就必須利用上班之餘再加強英文。然而，自我提升英文能力的方法有很多，其中「看影片學英文」，是一個既有趣又實用、彈性高、費用低的好方法。

為什麼「看外國影片」適合學習英文，因為影片中會出現各種角色及人物，而且有豐富的日常生活對白和故事，例如講電話、吃飯、社交、出差，甚至爭吵等，很多情節都近似自己周遭的生活。

「看影片學英文」是很多人曾建議加強英文的方法，但很少人真正能利用這個方法大幅提升英文能力，其一是看影片的初衷是娛樂，若要變成學習英文，樂趣便減少了，所以很少人有耐心再看第二遍、第三遍，從中學習原來不熟悉的英文句子並加以練習。

其二是市面上這類看影片學英文的書或工具，都是將一部電影的所有台詞一一羅列，並加以解析，但每部電影都有其探討的特殊主題，所以不熟悉的單字很多，因而造成學習阻礙，再者，有不少電影台詞其實也沒那麼實用，只是為了美化及加強電影的深度，因此，這個學習英文的方法便被大打折扣。

從影片中應學的重點

對於不是以英文為母語的人而言，英文永遠學不完，因此必須要有明確的目標。對於多數人而言，都是期望藉由英文能力提升，能在工作中有所助益或尋求更好的發展，因此，建議先以「職場英語」作為學習英文的首要目標，行有餘力再學習其他領域的英文。

透過看影片學英文，主要有三大部分，第一是學習一些非常口語，卻不容易在其他英文教材中看到的內容，例如在社交場合中，看到別

人懷孕時，想問對方「幾個月了」，若直接中翻英是：「How many months pregnant are you?」但老外不會這麼說，常用的問法是：「How far along are you?」

第二是從影片的台詞中，學到一些你原來不知道的說法，例如在電影《愛情失控點》中有句台詞：「You're wearing a new perfume.」（你擦新香水了。）原來中文的擦或噴香水的動詞應該用 wear，而不是噴農藥的 spray。還有當你打電話去電話中心投訴，動詞是用 file，例如在電影《翻轉幸福》中有句台詞：「I'm filing a complaint.」（我要投訴。）

第三是可以學到一些更優雅或隱喻的說法，例如在電影《飢餓遊戲》中，女主角說：「I am an open book.」（我沒有祕密。）這就比直接說：「I have no secret.」更加漂亮。還有在《搖搖欲墜》中，女主角對男主角說：「開工了。」她用的英文是：「Enter the dragon.」而不是平常我們通俗的說法：「Get to work.」。

除此之外，可以藉由影片了解西方文化，這是學習英文最難突破的地方，有時候一個句子中的每個單字都認識，卻不知道在某種場合中的意義為何？還有在影片中你會發現，西方人很重視打招呼、關心別人、回應別人，對他們而言，這是基本的禮貌，但在我們的眼中，可能會覺得有些話是多此一舉。

如何挑選適合的影片

以娛樂而言，任何你喜歡的影片都可以看，但是，從學習英文的角度，就得慎重選擇適合的影片。以我的學習經驗而言，有些影片值得記錄下來的內容不到 A4 的兩頁，像這種影片就不那麼合適，也不值得花時間再看一遍，比較合適的影片，多半可以記錄 A4 四頁以上的內容。當然，隨著你的英文程度愈來愈好，需要記錄的內容也會愈來愈少，那

就另當別論了。

　　一般而言，挑選影片可以遵循下列幾項要點：

　　一、不要挑選那些強調聲光效果的影片，例如一些英雄片《復仇者聯盟》、《鋼鐵人》等，大部分的時間都在打鬥，能學習的對話非常少，還有一些特殊影片如恐怖片、戰爭片、動作片、搞笑片等，這些也都很難學到太多的口語英文。

　　二、盡量挑選對話較多的影片，劇情的場景愈生活化愈好，裡面的台詞會更適合在工作或生活中使用，例如《拍賣家》、《搖搖欲墜》、《愛情失控點》等。

　　三、除了包含第二項的要素之外，內容若是和商業相關的更好，例如《高年級實習生》、《凸槌三人組》、《翻轉幸福》等，裡面的台詞與職場更加貼近，很多對話都是在職場中會出現的，學會後就可以直接使用。

　　再次強調，慎選影片很重要，其一是不會浪費時間，避免選到不適合的影片，看了兩、三遍還是學不到東西；其二是不會打擊信心，若挑選不夠實用的內容，光要記錄的單字及句子就多如牛毛，也會影響學習的意願。

看影片學英文三部曲

　　如前所述，光是把影片看過，對英文能力提升非常有限。曾經有位記者採訪我如何在職場中學習英文，她問我：「除了在工作的環境中學英文外，還有沒有其他有效的方法呢？」我回答：「看外國影片。例如《誰是接班人》（The Apprentice），就非常適合學習商用英文。」她接著問：「那你從影集中，學到哪些常用的英文句子？」當時我腦中浮現的只有大家耳熟能詳的那句：「You are fired.」其他的一時也想不起

來。於是我開始思考該如何觀看影片，才能真正提升自己的英文程度，以下是我得出的心得及注意事項，提供大家參考。

拜科技之賜，現在觀看影片的工具多樣且方便，包括DVD 播放器、平板電腦、手機、電腦等。和電腦相較，平板和手機可移動性高，缺點是螢幕較小，且選擇中英字幕的功能較不方便。和DVD相較，電腦還是比較方便。

原因有三：第一、使用電腦可以在書房或比較安靜的空間觀看，畢竟是在學習英語，最好不要受到干擾，而且有時需要大聲地練習（模仿口音及語調），也不會影響他人。第二、學習時必須停停走走，當你想停下來時，只要用滑鼠按一下「暫停」鍵就好了，把想學習的句子抄下來。再者，如果想回到前面的內容或快轉，電腦的操控性也比DVD來得方便；三、可以同時選擇兩種字幕（中文及英文），只要按滑鼠右鍵，把第二種字幕打勾，就會同時出現兩種字幕。

此外，影片的來源也要注意，當然第一是要找正版的影片，第二是要注意翻譯的水準，現在有不少中文翻譯都來自大陸，有些中文翻譯的不好或甚至是錯誤的。以下是「看影片學英文」的三部曲：

一部曲：先了解劇情

看第一遍時，先選中文字幕，目的是為了了解劇情，同時兼具娛樂效果，如果第一遍就選擇英文字幕或沒有字幕，保證看不到一半就會放棄，因為很多都看不懂，會很沮喪。英文程度較好的人，也可以在此步驟就同時選擇中英字幕，有些劇情就可以直接看英文字幕。

二部曲：練習「讀」及「寫」

當你看完第一遍，了解劇情後，再看第二遍時，這次就同時選擇中英字幕。此時主要在於學習英文如何表達，看到值得記錄的句子，就按

「暫停」鍵，把好句子的中英文都抄下來，之後再反覆練習。

切記，不要貪心，不要每字每句都想學，每個人的英文程度不同，為了維持學習的熱忱，只要挑選一些符合自己程度、重要且用得上的句子，畢竟影片的主要觀眾是以英語為母語的人，內容會有不少俚語，有些其實在職場上也很少會用到，學了也不容易記住。

當然，自己抄寫中英文句子很花時間，但好處是由自己篩選，且抄寫一次便會有印象。若懶得抄寫或打字速度不夠快，也可以上網去搜尋影片的劇本（script），但根據我的經驗，下載下來的劇本，由於內容太多，多半沒耐心看完。以前我也曾經把《六人行》和《慾望城市》的全部台詞都列印出來，但看了前面幾頁後，便沒耐心繼續看下去了。

因此，建議大家還是實事求是，按部就班的學習，英文程度一定是逐步累積的，想一步登天的人通常會半途而廢。

三部曲：第三遍練習「聽」及「說」

在上個步驟整理下來的句子，有空時就拿出來練習，光是讀只能增加一點記憶，必須大聲唸出來才能提升英語口語能力。有空時，可以再把影片看第三次，這次就不要顯示字幕，主要是訓練聽力。由於你對內容已經非常熟悉，聽到英文對話時，應該就可以直接了解其中含意了，這就做到和老外一樣，直接聽英語看影片，根本不需要字幕。

切記，在工作或社交場合中，有機會就要把學到的新句子拿出來使用，多使用幾次，這些句子就會植入腦中，爾後就不用思考，便能像講母語一樣，脫口而出。

總之，「看影片學英文」是一個非常有趣、有用且最容易持之以恆的方式。因為你可以在非常輕鬆和enjoy的狀況下，學到實用的口語英文，再搭配令人印象深刻的畫面，記憶會非常深刻。

本書記錄了五十部影片的重要台詞，讀者可以以此為基礎，接著再

利用相同的方法，不斷地蒐集一些常用的句子，一段時間後，你會發現自己會的口語英文愈來愈多，看影片的速度會愈來愈快，需要記錄的句子也會愈來愈少，而且再也不怕和外國人交談了，因為你會很有信心，這些句子都是你親自在影片中看過、聽過的。

第 **2** 章

你來我往不可少的
社交用語

試試看下列幾句常用的社交短句，如何用英文表達？

1. 你最近都在忙什麼？
2. 工作每天都差不多。
3. 久仰大名了！
4. 你不工作時都做些什麼？
5. 真不敢相信遇到了你。
6. 別跟我謙虛。
7. 很抱歉讓你久等了。
8. 這不合你的胃口嗎？
9. 今天由我為你們服務，想喝點什麼？
10. 不好意思，介意我們同桌嗎？

（答案在本章最後一頁）

Unit 1　見面問好，不只一種說法

　　平日打招呼是職場上最基本的禮儀，不論在哪個國家都一樣，但用英文打招呼，不要只會說：「How are you?」（你好嗎？）以及回答：「I'm fine. Thank you, and you?」（我很好，謝謝，你好嗎？）

情境模擬對話篇

A What have you been up to?
你最近都在忙什麼？

B Nothing much besides work.
除了工作外沒什麼。

A What's up, man?
老兄，你好嗎？

B Terrific.
好極了！

A Everything good?
都好嗎？

B Yup. Never better.
是的，好得很。

A How（are）you doing?
你好嗎？

B I am doing very well.
我很好。

A How's going?
最近如何？

B I am good.
我很好。

A How have you been?
你最近如何啊？

B I've never felt better.
好得不得了！

A Is work ok?
工作還好嗎？

B I've been all over the place.
我都忙壞了！

A How's it going?
進行得如何？

B It's going very well.
非常順利。

從電影對話中找靈感

▶ What have you been doing?
你在忙什麼？ .... 🎥 安諾瑪麗莎

▶ How have you been getting on?
你近來如何啊？ .... 🎥 布魯克林

▶ Long time no see.
好久不見。 .... 🎥 心靈大道

▶ Rough day?
今天很折騰吧！ .... 🎥 空中救援

▶ It's not my lucky day.
今天運氣不好。 .... 🎥 空中救援

▶ Are you alright?
你還好嗎？ .... 🎥 靈犬出任務

▶ Mostly fine.

大部分時間都好。··································· 🎥 我想念我自己

換種說法也可通

中譯	常用說法	另類說法
別挑毛病了。	Don't criticise it.	Don't knock it.《安諾瑪麗莎》
當然了。	Of course.	Damn straight.《安諾瑪麗莎》
開玩笑的。	Just kidding.	That was a joke.《驚天換日》
差一點。	That was close.	Close enough.《詭影任務》
他會很生氣。	He will be angry.	He's gonna be pissed.《白宮末日》
支持我。	Support me.	Get behind this.《白宮末日》
我答應你。	I promise.	You got my word.《白宮末日》

最容易運用的職場關鍵字　Man

　　口語英文常會說：「Hi, man!」（嗨，老兄！）Man這個字是「人；男人；老兄」的意思。

　　Man也常加在某個字的字尾，而變成一種職位，例如salesman（銷售人員）、fireman（消防人員），還有電影主角如Spiderman（蜘蛛人）、Ironman（鋼鐵人）等。Man的複數是men，若要特別強調女生時，則使用woman及women。

　　由man所衍生出來的字，常用的有manual, man-day, manpower及human。

　　Manual的意思是「手工的」，一般而言，大多數的交易都會盡量系統化，但有時因為成本考量，就會用手工做，manual做為名詞時的意思是「操作手冊；簡介」。

　　Man-day的意思是「工作日／人」，最常用在計畫開發系統，資訊部門會事先評估需要多少個man-day，假設需要60個man-day，一個人做

要60個工作天，若兩人一起做，就只要30個工作天。Manpower的意思是「人力」，例如我們常說：「我沒有足夠的manpower。」

　　Human 做為名詞意思是「人」，做為形容詞則為「人類的；人為的」，Human Resources的意思是「人力資源」，常把它做為「人事部門或人力資源部門」，縮寫就是HR。其他和man相關的用法請參閱以下例句。

1　Manual n. 手冊
Vicky will revise the operating manual accordingly.
薇琪將照著修改作業手冊。

2　Man-day n. 工作日／人
IT department estimated that it will take around 100 man-days to develop the new system.
資訊部門估計大約需要100（工作日／人）來開發新系統。

3　Manpower n. 人力
We are short of technical manpower.
我們缺乏技術人力。

4　Human adj. 人為的
This is not likely to be system issues but human errors.
這可能不是系統的問題，而是人為錯誤。

電影經典名言可以這樣應用

　　在《白日夢冒險王》中，主角是一位雜誌主編，上電視受訪時，當主持人問及他的緋聞，他回答：Where there's a smoke, there's fire. 在職場上，和同事聊到公司八卦時，例如聽說組織要重整或主管要被換掉了等，也可以用到這句話。

- **Where there's a smoke, there's fire.**
  無風不起浪。　　　　　　　　　　　　　　　　《白日夢冒險王》

Unit 2　七嘴八舌話家常

在公司裡經常有機會在某些場合和同事交流，例如生日宴會、慶功宴或老闆舉辦Town hall宣達一些事情，此時同事們可以藉此閒話家常、溝通公事或八卦一下。

情境模擬對話篇

A Hi, Annie. You got a new hairstyle.
嗨，安妮，妳換了個新髮型。

B How are you feeling?
你覺得如何呢？

A It's perfect for you.
這很適合妳。

B Thank you. It's so kind of you.
謝謝！你人真好！。

A How's work?
工作如何？

B Work was the same as every other day.
工作每天都差不多。

A Can I get you anything to drink?
妳要什麼飲料嗎？

B Slide me a soda please.
給我一瓶汽水，好嗎？

C Annie, come over here.
安妮，過來一下！

B Will you excuse me?
失陪一下！

C You want a beer?
要杯啤酒嗎？

B Love one.
當然。

C It is said that your boss is going to be replaced.
聽說妳老闆將被換掉了。

B Seriously? You blew me. There's been some chatter.
真的假的？你唬我！這是謠言罷了！

C Head hunter is looking for the replacement of this position in the market.
獵人頭公司已經在市場上找這個位置的替代人選了。

D Hey guys, what are you talking about?
嘿，伙計們，你們在聊什麼？

C Party's over. Gotta get back to work.
宴會結束了！得回去工作了。

從電影對話中找靈感

▶ I hope you get promoted.
我希望你升官。 ························ 🎥搖搖欲墜

▶ You're in a tough spot.
你的處境很艱難。 ······················ 🎥白宮風雲

▶ How's it coming?
進行得如何呢？ ························ 🎥愛情失控點

▶ She's half-kidding.
她是半開玩笑的。 ····················· 🎥愛情失控點

▶ Do you want to walk up with me?
你想陪我走過去嗎？ ………………………………… 🎥◀ 白日夢冒險王

▶ You are looking a little glum.
你看起來有點不開心。 ………………………………… 🎥◀ 愛情失控點

▶ Why are you in such a bad mood?
你怎麼心情這麼不好？ ………………………………… 🎥◀ 愛情失控點

▶ Don't say anything to anyone.
別把這事說出去。 …………………………………… 🎥◀ 丹林柯林斯

▶ I was wondering maybe we could get together sometime this
week.
我在想也許這周我們可以聚聚。 ……………………… 🎥◀ 心靈捕手

▶ When did you start working here?
你什麼時候開始在這裡工作？ ……………………… 🎥◀ 白宮風雲

▶ Have you heard this book?
你有聽過這本書嗎？ ………………………………………… 🎥◀ 人質

▶ The weather doesn't look so great.
天氣看起來不太好。 ………………………………… 🎥◀ 白日夢冒險王

▶ Are you kidding me?（Are you joking with me?）
你在跟我開玩笑嗎？ ………………………………… 🎥◀ 派特的幸福劇本

▶ Does this sound like a joke to you?
我像是在開玩笑嗎？ ………………………………… 🎥◀ 白宮末日

▶ I'm not superstitious.
我不迷信。 …………………………………………… 🎥◀ 派特的幸福劇本

▶ I don't mean to laugh.
我忍不住笑。 ………………………………………… 🎥◀ 驚天換日

▶ You have to watch your figure and you're right on the borderline.
你得注意身材，再下去就太胖。 …………………… 🎥◀ 實習大叔

▶ How is your blog coming along?
你的部落格寫得如何呢？ …………………………… 🎥◀ 白宮末日

▶ Piece of advice. It's not worth it.
給個建議，這不值得。……………………………… 🎥◀ 白宮末日

▶ Have you heard what's happening?
你知道發生什麼事嗎？……………………………… 🎥◀ 白宮末日

▶ I gotta use the bathroom.
我得去一下廁所。…………………………………… 🎥◀ 人質

▶ I'll get you coffee.
我去幫你拿咖啡。…………………………………… 🎥◀ 白宮風雲

▶ What are you doing on Friday night?
你星期五晚上有事嗎？……………………………… 🎥◀ 愛情失控點

▶ You seemed at such a low point.
你之前看起來很低潮。……………………………… 🎥◀ 愛情失控點

▶ We overheard some people talking about him.
我們偶然聽到一些人在談論他。…………………… 🎥◀ 愛情失控點

▶ Are you seeing somebody else?
你在和別人交往嗎？………………………………… 🎥◀ 愛情失控點

▶ What's your type?
你喜歡哪一型？……………………………………… 🎥◀ 機械姬

最容易運用的職場關鍵字 | Feel

現代人常說：「這裡沒有 fu！」其實就是取 feel（感覺；氣氛）的發音，fu 並不是英文單字的縮寫，只是台灣人發明的英文諧音，對 feel 的短縮拼法。

Feel 做為動詞的意思是「感覺；感受；認為」，例如：「How do you feel?」或「How are you feeling?」（你感覺如何呢？）口語中也常用 Feel 加上形容詞，用來表達當下的感受，例如 feel good（感覺良好）、feel strange（感覺奇怪）。

與 feel 相關的片語有 feel free 及 feel like。Feel free 意指「隨意；不

要客氣」，例如客人來家裡做客，可以對他說：「Feel free.」（請便）或「Feel free to stay here.」（在這裡不用客氣。）還有在email結尾時最常用的標準句子：「If you have any questions, please feel free to contact me.」（如果你有任何問題，請不要客氣與我聯絡。）

由feel衍生出來的字有feeling，意思是「感覺；感想；感情」，其他和feel相關的用法請參閱以下例句。

1 Feel v. 感覺；感受；認為
I feel I didn't properly articulate my argument.
我覺得我沒有適當地闡述我的爭論點。

2 Feel free ph. 隨意；不要客氣
Feel free to contact me if you need any clarification.
如果你需要任何澄清，不要客氣與我聯繫。

3 Feel like ph. 感覺好似；想要；意欲
My boss doesn't feel like discussing this issue.
我老闆不想討論這個問題。

4 Feeling n. 感覺；感想；感情
Honestly, your team is doing a good job but the feeling I get is that this team does it on isolation basis, with very little engagement with everyone else.
說實話，你的團隊做得不錯，但給我的感覺是，這個團隊是在孤立作業，很少接觸其他人。

Unit 3　外出參展的社交用語

　　在職場中，經常有機會到公司外面參加由廠商、行業公會或政府機關舉辦的說明會（seminar）、研討會（workshop）、會議（conference）等，可以藉此多認識些朋友及取得一些同業訊息。

情境模擬對話篇

B Hi, Joe. Appreciate you joining us.
嗨，喬伊，感謝您大駕光臨。

A I appreciate your inviting me to the seminar.
感謝你邀請我參加說明會。

B An honor finally to meet you. We've heard a lot about you.
終於有幸見到您了，久仰大名了！

A It's good to see you, too. I've heard so much about you.
我也很高興見到你。我對你早有耳聞了。

B May I have your business card?
能要張您的名片嗎？

A Sorry. Too busy talking. Here. It's my card.
抱歉，光顧著說話了！這是我的名片。

B Wow! Vice president! How many staff do you manage?
哇！副總裁！你底下管多少人啊？

A I have twenty staff under my crew.
我有二十個部屬。

B Do you enjoy working at ABC company?
你喜歡在 ABC 公司工作嗎？

A Yep, it's my passion.
是的，這是我的熱情所在。

B I'm really glad to hear that. Let me introduce one friend of mine to you. Hi, Vincent to see Joe.
很高興聽到你這麼說，讓我介紹一位朋友給你。嗨，文生來見過喬伊。

C Hi, Joe. Do we know each other from somewhere?
嗨，喬伊，我們是不是在哪裡見過面？

A Yeah, you look very familiar. It is possible we've met before.
是的，你看起來很眼熟，很可能我們以前見過。

C You're originally from Singapore?
你是新加坡本地人嗎？

A I am, born and raised.
我是土生土長的。

B I'm glad you had a chance to chat.
很高興你們有機會聊聊。

從電影對話中找靈感

▶ It's a beautiful day out there.
外面的天氣很好。 ⋯⋯⋯⋯⋯⋯⋯⋯⋯⋯⋯⋯⋯⋯ 🎥 通靈神探

▶ You're exactly like an old friend of mine.
你很像我一個老朋友。 ⋯⋯⋯⋯⋯⋯⋯⋯⋯ 🎥 時空永恆的愛戀

▶ Thanks for taking time out of your busy schedule.
謝謝你百忙中抽空出來。 ⋯⋯⋯⋯⋯⋯⋯⋯⋯⋯⋯ 🎥 驚爆焦點

▶ These events aren't really my strong suit.
在這些場合交際我不太擅長。 ⋯⋯⋯⋯⋯⋯⋯⋯⋯ 🎥 驚爆焦點

▶ It's nice to finally meet you.
很高興終於見到你。 ⋯⋯⋯⋯⋯⋯⋯⋯⋯⋯⋯⋯⋯ 🎥 命運鞋奏曲

▶ Maybe we can go out for coffee sometime.
也許有空我們可以出來喝杯咖啡。 …………………………………… 🎥 心靈捕手

▶ It's a real privilege for me.
這是我的榮幸。 ………………………………………………………………… 🎥 丹麥女孩

▶ Some things you never get used to.
有些事你永遠適應不了。 ……………………………………………………… 🎥 空中救援

▶ Robert has told me so much about you.
羅伯經常和我提到你。 ………………………………………………………… 🎥 拍賣家

▶ I'm happy you could be here today. (It's so good to have you here.)
很高興你們今天能來。 ………………………………………………………… 🎥 愛情失控點

▶ You are so not how I pictured you.
你和想像的完全不一樣。 ……………………………………………………… 🎥 白日夢冒險王

▶ We're glad you're here.
我們很高興你來了。 …………………………………………………………… 🎥 全面進化

▶ Terry speaks very highly of you.
泰瑞對你的評價很高。 ………………………………………………………… 🎥 因為愛你

換種說法也可通

中譯	常用說法	另類說法
明白了！	I've got it.	Gotcha.《搖搖欲墜》
再見！	See you.	See ya.《無處可逃》
您好！	How do you do?	Howdy.《高年級實習生》
乾杯！	Cheers!	Sláinte!《驚爆焦點》
你太棒了！	You were amazing.	You were fantastic.《拍賣家》
你今晚有什麼計畫？	Do you have plans tonight?	What do you up to tonight?《紙上城市》
稍等片刻。	Just a moment.	Shouldn't be a moment.《布魯克林》
右轉你就能看見。	Make a right and you can see it.	Make a right and you can't miss it.《因為愛你》

最容易運用的職場關鍵字　Appreciate

　　當你受到別人的恩惠或幫忙，想表達謝意時，可以用appreciate或thank，但這兩個字有些差異，appreciate的意思是「感激；感謝」，用在你非常了解這件事或物品的價值，就可以說Appreciate it或Much appreciated，感謝的力道比較強，而thank只是對別人的行動或給你好處時禮貌性地回應，比較是一般性的感謝。

　　Appreciate還有另一個意思是指土地、股票或貨幣的價格上升或增值，反義詞是depreciate，就是價格下跌或貶值，兩個字的名詞各為appreciation及depreciation，相關用法請參閱以下例句。

1 Appreciate v. 感謝；感激
I would appreciate if you can respond to my questions above ASAP.
如果你能盡快回應我上述的問題，我將不勝感激。

2 Appreciated adj. 感謝的；感激的
Your kind assistance and supports are highly appreciated.
非常感謝你仁慈的協助與支持。

3 Appreciation n. 升值
The appreciation of the dollar against the yen is on Japanese exports favor.
美元對日圓的升值對日本出口有利。

4 Depreciate v. 降價；跌價；貶值
YTD（Year-to-date）HTC's shares have depreciated for 40%.
年初至今宏達電股價已經下跌百分之四十。

Unit 4　與外國同事話家常

中文在世界上的地位愈來愈重要，很多老外也開始學中文，當他們看到華人面孔時，總喜歡摺幾句中文，你也可以藉此練練英文。

情境模擬對話篇

A Ni Hao.
你好！

B Wow! You speak some Mandarin.
哇！你會說中文。

A Just a little bit.
只會一點點！

B Where are you from?
你是哪裡人？

A Australian.
澳大利亞人。

B You don't sound like it.
聽你的口音不像。

A I grew up in the United States.
我在美國長大的。

B What do you do for living?
你是做什麼工作的？

A I am a real estate agent.
我是房地產經紀人。

B How'd you catch the real estate bug?
你是怎麼進入房地產這行的？

A Because I got an intern job in real estate company in college.
因為我在大學時就在房地產公司實習。

B How long have you had the job?
你做這工作多久了？

A Since graduation. It's about five years.
從畢業開始，大約五年了。

B What do you do when you're not working? You work out?
你不工作時都做些什麼？你健身嗎？

A Six days a week in a gym.
我每星期去六天健身房。

B Nice talking to you. I will see you sometime.
很高興和你談話，我們下次見了。

A I look forward to our next rendezvous.
期待我們下一次的會面。

從電影對話中找靈感

▶ I've been doing this for a long time.
我幹這一行很久了。 ……………………………… 🎥 翻轉幸福

▶ That's what we do.
這是我們的本行。 ……………………………… 🎥 聖母峰

▶ What do you ladies do for fun?
兩位女士有什麼愛好？ ……………………………… 🎥 安諾瑪麗莎

▶ Can I ask you a personal question?
可以問你一個私人問題嗎？ ……………………………… 🎥 命運鞋奏曲

▶ I love French and Italian the most.
我最喜歡法語和義大利語。 ……………………………… 🎥 安諾瑪麗莎

▶ It was nice getting to meet you ladies.
很高興認識妳們兩位女士。 ……………………………… 🎥 安諾瑪麗莎

▶ It was an honor spending time with you.
和你們在一起是我的榮幸。 ……………………………… 🎥 安諾瑪麗莎

▶ It's our great honor.
這是我們的榮幸。 …………………………………………… 🎥 無處可逃

▶ What year did you graduate?
你是哪一年畢業的？ ………………………………………… 🎥 非禮勿弒

電影經典名言可以這樣應用

　　台灣過去幾年曾發生很多事故，例食安事件、八仙塵爆、遊覽車火燒車等等，就非常適合用這句話，表示平時大家都不關切及嚴格監督，等到事情發生時，就開始互相指責及歸究責任。

• Sometimes it's easy to forget that we spend most of our time stumbling around the dark. Suddenly a light gets turned on and there's a fair share of blame to go around.
有時候我們很容易忘記大多數時候我們都是在黑暗中磕磕絆絆，突然間天亮了，人們卻開始互相指責起來。　　　　引自《驚爆焦點》

Unit 5　多些幽默讓氣氛更輕鬆

在電影《心靈捕手》中有一幕，主角麥克戴蒙（飾演一名失學的數學天才）感念羅賓威廉斯（飾演一名心理治療師）對他的啟蒙，最後兩人離別依依時，平時超矜持的麥克戴蒙，忍不住上前抱住羅賓威廉斯並說：「Hey, does this violate the patient-doctor relationship?」（嘿，這違反醫師病人關係嗎？）羅賓威廉斯幽默地回答：「Only if you grab my ass.」（除非你抓我屁股。）

「幽默」在西方文化中是很重要的特質，儘管在平時正式上班時，老外都不會忘了幽默，更何況在社交場合。

有次搭飛機出差，當時飛機已落地，大家取好行李等待下飛機，我手中提了好幾袋禮品，由於走道非常擁擠，在行走時我沒注意紙袋一直碰到前方老外的屁股，碰了兩、三次後，他忍不住回頭用眼神示意，我才發現並連忙道歉，他卻說：「You keep touching my ass, ...but I like it.」（你一直碰我屁股，……但是我喜歡。）

從電影對話中找靈感

▶ I'll take that as a compliment.
我會當這是讚美。 ⋯⋯⋯⋯⋯⋯⋯⋯⋯⋯⋯⋯⋯🎥 空中救援

▶ Don't go overboard.
別亂想了！ ⋯⋯⋯⋯⋯⋯⋯⋯⋯⋯⋯⋯⋯⋯⋯🎥 拍賣家

▶ Do you really think a bribe's gonna work?
你以為賄賂是有用的嗎？ ⋯⋯⋯⋯⋯⋯⋯⋯🎥 白宮末日

▶ That is burned in my memory.
我會記得一輩子的。 ⋯⋯⋯⋯⋯⋯⋯⋯⋯⋯⋯🎥 實習大叔

▶ Do I live up my profile or I do fall short?
我和我的簡介一致，還是不如簡介？ ·············· 翻轉幸福

▶ Don't play stupid. You can't pull it off.
別傻了，你贏不了的。 ·············· 史帝夫賈伯斯

▶ Will you sign this for me?
你能幫我簽名嗎？ ·············· 我想念我自己

▶ Quite the politician.
果然是政客。 ·············· 白宮末日

▶ I'll erase your brain later.
我待會給你清除記憶。 ·············· 搖搖欲墜

▶ It's fate.
這是命啊！ ·············· 通靈神探

▶ What's that look on your face?
你那是什麼表情？ ·············· 紙上城市

▶ Are you trying to communicate with me telepathically?
你打算心電感應我嗎？ ·············· 跨界失控

▶ What can I say?
我能說什麼呢？ ·············· 搖搖欲墜

▶ You're having fun with me.
你在開我玩笑。 ·············· 詭影任務

▶ How corrupt you are!
你真是貪官污吏啊！ ·············· 驚天換日

▶ You can eat my dust!
你望塵莫及吧！ ·············· 家有兩個爸

▶ Must've had surgery.
一定是整容。 ·············· 謎樣的雙眼

▶ You want my job?
你這是要搶我飯碗嗎？ ·············· 時空永恆的愛戀

▶ Do I look serious?
我不像認真的嗎？ ⋯⋯⋯⋯⋯⋯⋯⋯⋯⋯⋯⋯⋯⋯⋯⋯ 📹◀ 愛情沒有終點

▶ Did I just stutter?
我剛才有結巴嗎？ ⋯⋯⋯⋯⋯⋯⋯⋯⋯⋯⋯⋯⋯⋯⋯⋯ 📹◀ 謎樣的雙眼

▶ It wasn't a compliment.
這不是誇獎。 ⋯⋯⋯⋯⋯⋯⋯⋯⋯⋯⋯⋯⋯⋯⋯⋯ 📹◀ 時空永恆的愛戀

▶ He stole my line.
他偷學我的台詞。 ⋯⋯⋯⋯⋯⋯⋯⋯⋯⋯⋯⋯⋯⋯⋯⋯ 📹◀ 心靈捕手

▶ That's the worst joke I've ever heard in my entire life.
這是我這輩子聽過最難聽的笑話。 ⋯⋯⋯⋯⋯⋯ 📹◀ 時空永恆的愛戀

▶ Am I blushing right now?
我有點臉紅了？ ⋯⋯⋯⋯⋯⋯⋯⋯⋯⋯⋯⋯⋯⋯⋯⋯ 📹◀ 愛情失控點

▶ If you can't laugh, you're not having enough fun.
如果你笑不出來，表示你不夠幽默。 ⋯⋯⋯⋯ 📹◀ 白宮風雲

▶ I haven't lost my sense of smell.
我還沒失去嗅覺。 ⋯⋯⋯⋯⋯⋯⋯⋯⋯⋯⋯⋯⋯⋯⋯⋯ 📹◀ 45 年

▶ You know, there's a thing called the segue. It gets you from one
topic to the next one.
你知道有一種說法叫轉移話題，可以從一個話題轉移到另一個話題。
⋯⋯⋯⋯⋯⋯⋯⋯⋯⋯⋯⋯⋯⋯⋯⋯⋯⋯⋯⋯⋯⋯ 📹◀ 心靈大道

▶ So you've been telling some tall tales.
所以你一直在吹牛。 ⋯⋯⋯⋯⋯⋯⋯⋯⋯⋯⋯⋯⋯⋯ 📹◀ 家有兩個爸

▶ I mean that as a compliment from the bottom of my heart.
這是我發自內心的讚賞。 ⋯⋯⋯⋯⋯⋯⋯⋯⋯⋯⋯⋯ 📹◀ 家有兩個爸

換種說法也可通

中譯	常用說法	另類說法
任你差遣。	Being of service.	I am all yours.《大夢想家》
我什麼都沒說。	I didn't say anything.	I swallowed a bug.《心靈捕手》
我不知所措。	I am at a loss.	I froze.《家有兩個爸》
你好！	Hello!	Hey there.《人質》
他還好嗎？	Is he ok?	What's he up to?《聖母峰》
開玩笑的！	Just kidding.	That was a joke.《驚天換日》
很高興認識你。	Nice to meet you.	Super to make your acquaintance.《家有兩個爸》
我不認得你。	I can't recognize you.	I can't place you.《非禮勿弒》

電影經典名言可以這樣應用

　　當公司要尋找新進員工，希望能尋找有創新能力、思維獨特，而不是墨守成規的組員時，或許你可以以這句話跟人資部說明自己的要求。

- **I thought the goal was to find people with a different way of thinking.**
我認為目標是尋找思維獨特的人。　　　　　　　引自《實習大叔》

Unit 6　多年未見的見面用語

　　參加外部活動時，有時會不期而遇多年不見的同事、同學或朋友，此時總有說不完的話，問候對方及家人近況，甚至聊到一些共同認識的朋友。

情境模擬對話篇

A Hey, Michael. What a coincidence!
嘿，邁可，真巧啊！

B Betty, I can't believe I bumped into you.
貝蒂，真不敢相信遇到了妳。

A It's been ages.
好久不見！

B It's been a while. I don't hardly recognize you.
好久不見了！我幾乎認不出妳了！

A Elegant as ever.
還是這麼帥！

B As beautiful as ever, so sexy.
妳也是一樣美麗，一樣有魅力。

A How long have we known each other?
我們認識多久了？

B Quite a while. It goes so fast.
挺久了！時間過得真快！

A How are the wife and kids?
老婆小孩都好嗎？

B They are all good. I appreciate your concern.
他們都很好，謝謝妳的關心！

A Give my best to your wife.
代我向你老婆問好。

B Thank you. Emma told me you're thriving. You have no idea how pleased I am for you.
謝謝！艾瑪告訴我妳發展得很好，妳不知道我有多麼為妳開心。

A I am flattered. Just earning a living
我受寵若驚，只是維持生計而已。

B You're always being modest. Got a pen?
妳總是那麼謙虛。有筆嗎？

A Yes. Here you go.
有，給你。

B Here's my number. I hope we keep in touch.
這是我的電話號碼，希望我們保持聯絡。

A Sure thing.
沒問題。

最容易運用的職場關鍵字　Go

　　Go 主要的意思有「去；走；從事；變成」，常用的句型是後面加上形容詞，例如 go wrong（失敗；出毛病）、go crazy（發瘋；失去理智）。還有後面加上原形動詞，例如：「Let's go get some drinks.」（我們去拿一些飲料。）

　　與 go 相關的片語有很多，go through 的意思是「被正式通過；順利完成；討論」，例如 Go through the proposal（討論一下提案）。Go into 的意思是「進入某事情」，例如 go into details（詳盡描述；進入細節）。Go live 常用在系統上線，也可以用在新事業或新產品上線。

由go衍生出來的字有ongoing及going forward.。Ongoing意思是「前進的；正在進行的；不間斷的」，常用在形容持續的交易、活動或支援。Going forward的意思是「接下來；展望未來」，常放在句首做為發語詞，一般聽到going forward，後面就是要表達的重點了，其他和go相關的用法請參閱以下例句。

1 Going forward ph. 接下來
Going forward, please have her perform the same task every week.
接下來請讓她每週執行相同的任務。

2 Go through ph. 順利完成；討論
Vivian, arrange time for me to go through with Kevin later.
薇薇安，待會安排時間讓我和凱文討論一下。

3 Go live ph. 上線
Taiwan is ready for new business go live.
台灣已經準備好讓新業務上線了。

4 Go into details ph. 詳細描述
You need not go into details.
你不必詳細描述。

電影經典名言可以這樣應用

當進行一些具風險性的計畫或投資時，這句話也可以派上用場。

• **People fear what they don't understand. They always have.**
人們因無知而恐懼，一向如此。　　　　　　　　　引自《全面進化》

Unit 7 到外國友人家作客

　　老外的生活很單純，不會像台灣人常去外面聚餐、唱KTV、喝酒，他們的社交活動多半也是在家裡舉行，所以偶爾會有機會到老外的同事或老闆家作客，也要能夠閒話家常。

情境模擬對話篇

A Hi, Andy. Welcome! Have trouble finding the place?
嗨，安迪，歡迎！這邊很難找嗎？

B My GPS took me the long way. Sorry, I'm a little late.
我的衛星定位導航系統帶我繞遠路。抱歉，有點遲到。

A It's okay.
沒關係。

B I brought you a present.
給你帶了禮物。

A Oh, very sweet of you. Come in and let me take the tour.
喔，你真好！進來吧，我帶你參觀一下。

B This is lovely. It makes very good use of the space. You have good taste.
很漂亮！空間利用得很好。你的品味不錯啊！

A That's a really big compliment. Make yourself at home.
真是很大的誇獎。當成自己的家。

B Food smells so good here.
這些食物看起來好好吃喔！

A I'm not that great in cook.
我不是很擅長料理。

B Don't play humble fame with me.
別跟我謙虛。

A Let's all take our seat. Here we go.
大家都就座，開動了！

邊吃邊聊

A Do you want a soda?
你要喝汽水嗎？

B No, thank you, I'm good. Time to go.
不了，謝謝！該走了！

A Stick around a minute.
再留一會兒嘛！

B I'm bothering you so long. Thank you for having me over. It's very nice.
我打擾你們太久了，謝謝你邀請我來，很盡興。

A If you want to come by, you are always welcome.
如果你想過來，我們隨時歡迎你！

從電影對話中找靈感

▶ I wanted to thank you for including me to such a delicious feast.
我想感謝你邀請我加入這麼美味的一餐。 .... 搖搖欲墜

▶ I'm truly overjoyed.
我真的很喜歡。 .... 時空永恆的愛戀

▶ This is a conversation for another time.
以後再聊這個話題吧！ .... 非禮勿弒

▶ You know how overjoyed I am?
你知道我有多開心嗎？ .... 🎥◀ 搖搖欲墜

▶ Will you give Andrew a tour of the place?
你願意帶安德魯參觀這地方嗎？ .... 🎥◀ 搖搖欲墜

▶ Let the man wipe his boots off.
趕緊讓他就座吧！ .... 🎥◀ 搖搖欲墜

▶ I had one too many wine.
我喝太多酒了。 .... 🎥◀ 非禮勿弒

▶ I'm so happy you could join us.
你能來真是太好了。 .... 🎥◀ 安諾瑪麗莎

▶ It's so intrusive.
打擾了。 .... 🎥◀ 與外婆同行

▶ We're having a wonderful time.
我們很開心。 .... 🎥◀ 靈犬出任務

▶ This is some place. This is like a mansion. Very classical.
這裡真不錯！簡直是座豪宅，非常經典！ .... 🎥◀ 搖滾女王

換種說法也可通

中譯	常用說法	另類說法
開動吧！	Here we go.	Let's dig in. 《搖搖欲墜》
請自便！	Suit/Help yourself.	Knock out yourself. 《搖搖欲墜》
請別拘束！	Please feel free.	Make yourself comfortable. 《時空永恆的愛戀》
她在等我。	She's waiting for me.	She's expecting me. 《謎樣的雙眼》

最容易運用的職場關鍵字　Find

　　在職場上，經常會聽到老闆告訴部屬：「Go find out.」（去搞清楚。）或「Find out more.」（去了解更多。）

　　Find的意思有「發現；找到；得到」，這個字雖然很簡單，但在email的使用率卻非常高，例如：「Please find the attached file.」（請看附加的文件。）還有「I trust that this email finds you well.」（我相信你一切安好），常用在email的開頭，寫給久未聯絡的人。

　　和find相關的片語，最重要的就是find out，意思是「搞清楚；查明真相」，例如：「I'll find out in a few days.」（過幾天就知道了。）由find衍生出來的字有finding，意思是「調查結果；發現」，職場中常見的是audit findings，意思就是「稽核結果」，其他和find相關的用法請參閱以下例句。

---

1 Find v. 找到；發現
We have discussed internally and please find my feedback as below.
我們已經內部討論了，請看我的回饋如下。

---

2 Find v. 找到；發現
I'm just finding my way around.
我還在熟悉中。

---

3 Find out ph. 搞清楚；查明真相
Can you find out and let me know the details?
你能查清楚並讓我知道細節嗎？

---

4 Finding n. 調查結果；發現
As discussed in yesterday audit finding review meeting, please elaborate further for the monitoring mechanism.
如同昨天在稽核結果審查會議上的討論，請進一步闡述監督機制。

百用句型

- Would you like _____ ?
  你想要 _____ 嗎？
  ①a glass of wine（杯酒）；
  ②a cup of tea（杯茶）；
  ③a glass of water（杯水）

電影經典名言可以這樣應用

這句話可以拆開使用，用來鼓勵別人或在社交時使用。

- **To see the world, things dangerous to come to, to see behind walls, to draw closer, to find each other and to feel, that is the purpose of life.**
  開拓視野、突破萬難、看見世界、身歷其境、貼近彼此、感受生活，這就是生活的目的。　　　　　　　　　　引自《白日夢冒險王》

Unit 8 | 把讚美的話語常掛嘴邊

「讚美」在西方文化中是很重要的要素，平時在教育小孩時，外國的父母和老師總是讚美多過於責罵，所以長大後到職場，他們也經常把讚美掛在嘴邊，不像是東方文化，總是以責罵為主，導致讚美的話，通常都說不出口。

在外商工作時，外籍老闆經常把well done, good job, fantastic, excellent等讚美的話掛在嘴邊。當我聽到老闆這麼對我說時，都會感到無限的榮耀，誓言一定要拚命工作，以報答老闆，現在想想還真傻，其實那也只是他們的口頭禪而已。

既然一、兩句簡單的讚美，能換得部屬及同事的賣力及協助，何樂而不為呢？在社交場合中，更應該把讚美運用到極致。

從電影對話中找靈感

▶ It looks marvelous on you.
穿在你身上真美。 …………………………………………… 📹 拍賣家

▶ You look incredible.
你看起來好極了。 …………………………………………… 📹 派特的幸福劇本

▶ You're really slimming down.
你真的瘦了！ …………………………………………… 📹 實習大叔

▶ You are so pretty. I like your hair today.
你真漂亮，我喜歡你今天的髮型。 …………………… 📹 愛情失控點

▶ Work it!
真有你的！ …………………………………………… 📹 愛情沒有終點

▶ Pretty fancy.
厲害啊！ ·· 愛情沒有終點

▶ What a nice voice you have!
你的聲音很好聽！ ······························· 翻轉幸福

▶ That's going to be some good writing.
一看文筆就很好。 ······························· 搖搖欲墜

▶ Pretty impressive.
這很厲害。 ·· 加州大地震

▶ You look terrific.
你看起來很美。 ···································· 白宮風雲

▶ It's magnificent.
太美了！ ·· 詭影任務

▶ You have a miraculous voice.
你的聲音非常的優美。 ·························· 安諾瑪麗莎

▶ It's very scientific.
非常專業。 ··· 我想念我自己

▶ You're pretty something.
你很出色。 ··· 紙上城市

▶ Work your magic.
妙手回春。 ··· 命運鞋奏曲

▶ You look so beautiful.
你看起來真美！ ·································· 通靈神探

換種說法也可通

中譯	常用說法	另類說法
妳懷孕多久了？	How long have you been pregnant?	How far along are you? 《我想念我自己》
預產期什麼時候？	When will you give a birth?	When are you due? 《愛睡在一起》
她很特別。	She is special.	She's one in million. 《宵禁》
這世界真小。	It's a small world.	The world is a small place. 《布魯克林》

電影經典名言可以這樣應用

這句話可以應用在一般社交場合中。

- **There was a saying in Italy "Years, lovers and glasses of wine these are things that you never be count".**
  義大利有句老話：「歲月、愛人和美酒，這些是無法以數計的美好。」
  引自《時空永恆的愛戀》

Unit 9 　陪外國客戶外出用餐

　　在外商工作，經常會有國外的同事或老闆視察業務、稽核或政令宣導等，此時就必須帶他們到外面餐廳吃飯。

情境模擬對話篇

A I'm so sorry to keep you waiting.
很抱歉讓你久等了。

B It's OK. I just arrived. It's busier here than I would've thought.
沒關係，我剛到，沒想到人這麼多。

A The food must be very tasty.
食物一定很美味。

B Excuse me. We're ready to order.
不好意思！可以點菜了。

C What can I get you?
你們要點什麼？

B I'll have the creamed spinach over poached egg. And a dry Martini. With an olive.
我要一份奶油菠菜水煮蛋，和一杯乾馬丁尼，加一個橄欖。

A I'll have the same.
我要一樣的。

B You are vegetarian as well?
你也吃素嗎？

A No, I'll eat everything.
不，我什麼都吃。

B What do you do on Sundays?
你周日都做些什麼？

A Nothing in particular. But I'm working on a book recently.
沒什麼特別的，不過我最近在寫一本書。

B What's it about?
是關於什麼的？

A It's about children education.
是關於孩子教育。

B Wow! How old are your children? Do you have any pictures?
哇！你的孩子多大了？你有照片嗎？

A I only have one girl and she is 11. This is my family photo.
我只有一個十一歲的女兒，這是我們全家的照片。

B She is lovely and looks like you. Around the eyes.
她很可愛，長得像你，眼睛這裡。

A Thank you.
謝謝。

從電影對話中找靈感

▶ I hear the finest restaurant in Moscow is across the street.
我聽說莫斯科最棒的餐廳就在對街。 ⋯⋯⋯⋯⋯⋯ 🎥 詭影任務

▶ Could I see a menu, please?
可以給我看一下菜單嗎？ ⋯⋯⋯⋯⋯⋯⋯⋯⋯ 🎥 白宮風雲

▶ What would you suggest?
有什麼推薦的菜嗎？ ⋯⋯⋯⋯⋯⋯⋯⋯⋯⋯ 🎥 白宮風雲

▶ Would you like an appetizer before your meal?
在正餐之前您要來個開胃菜嗎？ ⋯⋯⋯⋯⋯⋯ 🎥 大賣空

▶ What would you like for your main dish?
您想吃什麼主菜嗎？ ⋯⋯⋯⋯⋯⋯⋯⋯⋯⋯ 🎥 白宮風雲

▶ you like your coffee with your dinner or later?
請問您的咖啡是隨餐送來，或稍後再送呢？ ⋯⋯⋯⋯⋯ 📹 安諾瑪麗莎

▶ How did you learn to eat spaghetti like that?
你在哪學這樣吃義大利麵的？ ⋯⋯⋯⋯⋯⋯⋯⋯⋯ 📹 布魯克林

▶ Do you wanna share this?
想分一點嗎？ ⋯⋯⋯⋯⋯⋯⋯⋯⋯⋯⋯⋯⋯⋯ 📹 派特的幸福劇本

▶ Will it take long? Not long. They'll be ready in a few minutes.
要等很久嗎？不會很久，幾分鐘就好了。 ⋯⋯⋯⋯⋯ 📹 白宮風雲

▶ Can I get that out of the way for you?
要我幫你收掉這盤子嗎？ ⋯⋯⋯⋯⋯⋯⋯⋯⋯⋯ 📹 搖搖欲墜

▶ Everything's great.
一切都很好。 ⋯⋯⋯⋯⋯⋯⋯⋯⋯⋯⋯⋯⋯⋯⋯ 📹 靈犬出任務

▶ Your purse is vibrating. Check your phone?
你的包包在震動。要看一下手機嗎？ ⋯⋯⋯⋯⋯⋯ 📹 搖滾女王

▶ I'll just get the check then.
我直接結帳吧！ ⋯⋯⋯⋯⋯⋯⋯⋯⋯⋯⋯⋯⋯⋯ 📹 安諾瑪麗莎

最容易運用的職場關鍵字 | Think

　　開會時，當你想再次確認別人的意見，可以問：「You think so?」（你這麼認為嗎？）或當你反對別人的意見時，可以說：「I don't think so.」（我不這麼認為。）

　　Think常解釋為「想；認為」，例如：「Think out of the box.」（跳出框架思考。）也可以用「Think outside the box.」意思就是可以自由地去思考，不要畫地自限，不要被舊有的規則或慣例所約束或侷限。

　　Thought有兩種用法，在前文會話中是做為think的過去分詞，但也可以做為名詞，意思是「想法；見解」，例如同事問你：「Your thoughts?」（你的想法呢？）你回答：「I don't have any thoughts on it.」（這事我沒有任何想法。）

Thinking 的意思是「思想；思考」，例如我們常鼓勵別人要 Positive thinking（正向思考），其他和 think 相關的用法請參閱以下例句。

1 Think **V.** 想；思考；認為
You won't come up with good ideas until you think out of the box.
你不會想出好主意，直到你跳出框架思考。

2 Think of **ph.** 想像；思考；想到
We need to think of the practicalities and what we can do.
我們需要考慮可行性和我們能做些什麼。

3 Think about **ph.** 考慮；考量
Will you at least think about the idea of making a change?
你是否至少考慮做一點改變的想法？

4 Think through **ph.** 徹底想清楚
You must always think a problem through before acting.
在採取行動之前，你必須把問題徹底想清楚。

5 Thinking **n.** 思想；思考
It is important to have a good and progressive thinking team in this area.
在這方面，有一個良好和進步思想的團隊是很重要的。

Unit 10　邊吃邊聊話題多

　　午休時間或下班後，三五同事一起用餐是常有的事，尤其是晚上，就有較多時間可以閒話家常，用力地八卦一下或互吐工作心聲。

情境模擬對話篇

A I'm starved.
我餓死了。

B What will you have? Who wants some appetizers?
你們要吃什麼？誰要吃開胃菜？

C Bill, could you help us order then we can share?
比爾，你可以幫大家點菜，然後我們一起分享嗎？

W May I take your order? Would you like to start with something to drink?
你們要點菜了嗎？要不要先來點喝呢？

All I'd like a glass of iced tea. Make it two. I'll just have water.
我要一杯冰紅茶。來兩杯吧。我只要水就好了。

用餐中

B Was it not to your taste?
這不合你的胃口嗎？

C It's a little heavy.
口味有點重。

A They don't taste so good.
味道不怎麼樣。

W Anything else I can get you, sir?
先生，你們還需要別的嗎？

B I think we're all set with food. Do you do free refills here?
我想我們的食物夠了，這裡可以免費續杯嗎？

W Free refills on soft drinks or coffee except on alcohol.
除了酒，飲料和咖啡都可以免費續杯。

All I'll have the same again. Me too. More water, please.
再給我來一杯。我也要。麻煩加點水。

W Back in a minute.
馬上就來。

B Let me pick up the check today.
今天讓我埋單吧！

A No. Let's slice the pie three ways.
不要啦！三人分攤吧！

B Could we have the bill, please?
我們要埋單了。

W That's 100 on the card and you can add whatever tip.
共 100 美元、信用卡付帳，你可以在上面加任何小費。

從電影對話中找靈感

▶ I'm starved. Let's get some food.
我很餓了，我們去吃點東西！ ························· 📽◀ 出棋制勝

▶ I'm getting in shape.
我要減肥。 ······································ 📽◀ 派特的幸福劇本

▶ I'm not ready to order yet.
我還沒想好要點什麼。 ······················· 📽◀ 白宮風雲

▶ Could you come back in a few minutes?
你能幾分鐘後再過來嗎？ ···················· 📽◀ 加州大地震

▶ Can I tell you about our specials?
我能介紹一下我們的特色菜嗎？ ………………………… 🎥 加州大地震

▶ I love that you order for me.
我喜歡你為我點的。 …………………………………… 🎥 愛情失控點

▶ Will you have one with me?
想和我喝一杯嗎？ ……………………………………… 🎥 白宮風雲

▶ That is something, huh?
味道很不錯吧？ ………………………………………… 🎥 天菜大廚

▶ I've not eaten it.
我沒吃過。 ……………………………………………… 🎥 布魯克林

▶ No, I'm stuffed. I'm ready for the check.
不，我很飽了。我準備要埋單了。 …………………… 🎥 白宮風雲

▶ Let's just split it. Go Dutch.
讓我們分擔吧！各付各的！ …………………………… 🎥 實習大叔

最容易運用的職場關鍵字　Except

　　一般而言，公司都有內部政策、規範或流程，但有時為了因應客戶需求或市場競爭，會需要例外（exception）處理。有次老闆說：「從今天開始，凡是單筆費用超過一千美元，都必須拿給我簽核，沒有例外（No exception）。」

　　Except常和介系詞for一起使用，變成except for，意思和except相同，那麼兩者有何不同呢？基本上，如果後面接的是名詞，兩者都可以使用，但如果後面接的是附屬子句、介系詞或連接詞，就只能用except，例如：「He's good-looking except when he smiles.」（除了笑之外，他是很好看的。）

　　由except所衍生出來的字有exceptional及exception。當你需要尋求exception的核准，最適合的動詞是grant（同意；允許），例如：「This exception is granted.」（這個例外已被允許）及「CEO has granted some

exceptions.」（執行長已經允許幾個例外了），其他和except相關的用法請
參閱以下例句。

1 Except prep. 除了……之外
Everybody can attend except you.
所有人都可以參加除了你。

2 Exception n. 例外
I have no authority to grant exceptions to this requirement.
我沒有權利同意這個例外的要求。

3 Except for ph. 除了……之外
I have accepted most of the changes except for this.
我已經接受了大部分的變更，除了這個之外。

4 Exceptional adj. 例外的
There is exceptional handling of process for delayed transactions.
有一個對於延遲交易的例外處理流程。

百用句型

• Can you get me _____ ?
可以給我 _____ 嗎？

①a glass of water（一杯水）；
②some tissue（一些紙巾）；
③some chili sauce（一些辣椒醬）；
④a place setting for child（一套兒童餐具）

Unit 11　下班後的小酌歡聚

　　上班很鬱悶，下班時三五同事找個酒吧喝點小酒，是解除壓力的一種好方式。

情境模擬對話篇

A Let's sit over here.
我們坐這邊。

B Come here often?
常來嗎？

A No. I come here a bit. From time to time.
沒有，我很少來這裡。偶爾吧！

W My name is Lucy. I'll be taking care of you today. What would you like to drink?
我叫露西，今天由我為你們服務，想喝點什麼？

A I'll have a vodka with 7Up, please.
請給我一杯伏特加酒加七喜汽水。

B I'll have a double scotch.
我要雙份的蘇格蘭酒。

W Coming up.
馬上就好！

邊喝邊聊

B Bottoms up.（Loud）
乾杯！（大聲的）

A Keep your voice down.
小聲一點。

W Would you like anything else?
你還想要點什麼嗎？

B Anthony, how's that vodka tasting?
安東尼，你那伏特加味道如何？

A It's good. I'd like another one, please.
很好。我想要再來一杯。

B I'll have one of those.
我也要一杯。

W Sure thing.
沒問題。

A This one's on me.
這杯我請。

B Thanks. I'm gonna go use the facility.
謝了！我去趟洗手間。

A Are you okay?
你還好嗎？

B No problem. Just need to pee.
沒問題。只是需要去尿尿。

從電影對話中找靈感

▶ Excuse me, mind if we join you.
不好意思，介意我們同桌嗎？ ·················· 🎥 高年級實習生

▶ Your waiter will be here in a minute to take your order.
服務生馬上過來為您點菜。 ·················· 🎥 搖滾女王

▶ Drink as many as you want. On me.
儘管喝吧，我請客！ ·················· 🎥 丹林柯林斯

▶ Did you just hit on the waitress?
你剛剛在把服務生嗎？ ⋯⋯⋯⋯⋯⋯⋯⋯⋯⋯⋯⋯⋯⋯⋯⋯ 🎥◀ 實習大叔

▶ Do you have a to go cup?
你們有外帶杯嗎？ ⋯⋯⋯⋯⋯⋯⋯⋯⋯⋯⋯⋯⋯⋯⋯⋯⋯⋯ 🎥◀ 實習大叔

▶ Put it on my tab.
算在我帳上。 ⋯⋯⋯⋯⋯⋯⋯⋯⋯⋯⋯⋯⋯⋯⋯⋯⋯⋯⋯⋯ 🎥◀ 心靈捕手

▶ We'd like the bill, please.
麻煩埋單。 ⋯⋯⋯⋯⋯⋯⋯⋯⋯⋯⋯⋯⋯⋯⋯⋯⋯⋯⋯⋯⋯ 🎥◀ 白宮風雲

▶ Spilt the check.
各付各的。 ⋯⋯⋯⋯⋯⋯⋯⋯⋯⋯⋯⋯⋯⋯⋯⋯⋯⋯⋯⋯⋯ 🎥◀ 詭影任務

▶ How much do I owe you?
我該給你多少錢？ ⋯⋯⋯⋯⋯⋯⋯⋯⋯⋯⋯⋯⋯⋯⋯⋯⋯ 🎥◀ 愛情失控點

▶ Can I have a receipt, please?
可以開收據嗎？

最容易運用的職場關鍵字　Up

　　Up 做為副詞的意思是「向上；在上面；上揚」，這個字小學生應該都會，那為什麼要特別強調這個字呢？原因是 up 在商用英文中常出現，而且有時候不容易了解它的意思為何？例如在口語中常出現「What are you up to?」（你在做什麼呢？）及「Time's up.」（時間到了。）

　　與 up 相關的片語有不少，例如 screw up 的意思是「搞砸」，常用在警告或責怪同事或部屬。Mix up 的意思是「弄混；搞亂」，若把兩個字合起來 mix-up，就變成名詞，意思是和動詞相同。Come up 的意思是「發生；出現」，當別人問你何時才能到，可以回覆：「Coming up.」（馬上就來。）

　　由 up 所衍生出來的字相當多，up to 的意思是「視為某人的責任；勝任；參與」，例如「It's up to you.」（由你決定或隨便你）。Upfront 的意思是「預付的；前收的」，例如你購買某些投資商品，必須先支付 upfront fee（預付費用），其他和up相關的用法請參閱以下例句。

1 Mix-up n. 弄錯；搞亂
There's been some mix-up with my reservation.
我的訂位弄錯了。

2 Screw up ph. 搞砸
Don't screw this up.
別搞砸了。

3 Come up ph. 發生；出現
We've got spring break coming up.
我們馬上就要放春假了。

4 Up to ph. 參與
I know you're up to something.
我知道你們在搞鬼。

5 Up to date ph. 流行的；最新的
Up to date we have no news of his arrival.
到目前為止，我們沒有他到達的消息。

百用句型

- How would you like your _____?
  您希望 _____ 怎麼做呢？
  ①egg（蛋）；
  ②steak（牛排）；
  ③sandwich（三明治）

解答／十句常用社交英文的英譯

1. What have you been up to?
2. Work was the same as every other day.
3. We've heard a lot about you.
4. What do you do when you're not working?
5. I can't believe I bumped into you.
6. Don't play humble fame with me.
7. I'm so sorry to keep you waiting.
8. Was it not to your taste?
9. I'll be taking care of you today. What would you like to drink?
10. Excuse me, mind if we join you?

第 **3** 章

開會談判不可少的
關鍵用語

試試看下列幾句開會談判常用的句子，如何用英文表達？

1. 他的話的確有道理。
2. 這不是優先處理的事。
3. 你打算怎麼做？
4. 這對我有什麼好處？
5. 你這是在小題大做。
6. 你幹嘛那麼盛氣凌人？
7. 不是針對你。
8. 這是千載難逢的好機會。
9. 我們握手說定了。
10. 你們似乎在敲詐我們。

（答案在本章最後一頁）

Unit 1　開場有效率的英文會議

　　開會的環節不外乎開場、報告主題、表達意見、反應（正面、負面、中性）、挑戰、質疑、詢問、解釋等，學好相關常用的句子，才能在英文會議中表現得宜。

情境模擬對話篇

H Let's take our seats. Where is Babson?
大家請坐，巴布森在哪裡？

A He was gonna sit in, possibly, but he's not gonna be able to make it today.
他本來能參加這個會，但他今天無法參加了。

H We'll get started.
我們開始吧！

B Let's brief you on the agenda today.
讓我先講一下今天開會的議程。

B Now, then, the first thing we need to talk about the compensation for customers.
現在，第一件事我們要談的是客戶補償的事。

H Everybody has an opinion on this?
你們想要發表什麼意見嗎？

C I thought it was very reasonable thing to do.
我認為這件事非常合理。

D It's fine by me.
我沒意見。

E I don't think it's quite as simple as that.
我覺得問題沒那麼簡單。

F It can't be that easy.
沒那麼容易。

G Sorry, if I can chip in.
抱歉，如果我可以插話的話。

H Go ahead.
說吧！

G Let's think about this from customer angle, not company.
讓我們從客戶的角度考量，而不是公司。

D He does make a valid point.
他的話的確有道理。

H We'll take a ten-minute break.
我們休息十分鐘。

Keep debating

H Let's stop there for now. To be continued.
我們今天就到這裡吧！未完待續！

從電影對話中找靈感

▶ The position was already filled.
這位子已經被人佔了。 ⋯⋯⋯⋯⋯⋯⋯⋯⋯⋯ 🎥 謎樣的雙眼

▶ If you can tell me your name if we go around. That'll be helpful.
如果你們能逐一介紹自己，那就再好不過了。 ⋯⋯⋯⋯ 🎥 驚爆焦點

▶ Do you want to say something?
你想先說幾句嗎？ ⋯⋯⋯⋯⋯⋯⋯⋯⋯⋯⋯⋯⋯ 🎥 驚爆焦點

▶ Let's get started.
我們開始吧！ ⋯⋯⋯⋯⋯⋯⋯⋯⋯⋯⋯⋯⋯⋯⋯ 🎥 心靈捕手

▶ We apologize. We're running a bit late today.
抱歉，我們來遲了一點。 …………………………………… 🎬◀ 白宮風雲

▶ I'm late for something.
我有些事耽擱了。 …………………………………………… 🎬◀ 高年級實習生

▶ Did I hijack the session?
我搶話了嗎？ …………………………………………………… 🎬◀ 大賣空

▶ I don't want to interrupt the proceedings.
不好意思要打擾大家。 ………………………………………… 🎬◀ 布魯克林

▶ Can I say something here?
可以容我說幾句嗎？ …………………………………………… 🎬◀ 驚爆焦點

▶ Am I interrupting?
我可以打斷嗎？ ………………………………………………… 🎬◀ 愛情沒有終點

▶ Sorry, didn't mean to interrupt.
抱歉，無意打斷。 ……………………………………………… 🎬◀ 高年級實習生

▶ Would you excuse me for a moment?
我可以失陪一下嗎？ …………………………………………… 🎬◀ 白宮風雲

▶ That's it for today.
今天到此為止。 ………………………………………………… 🎬◀ 心靈捕手

最容易運用的職場關鍵字　Valid

　　當別人提出觀點，而你是認同的，可以回覆：「Your points are valid.」（你的論點是令人信服的）或簡單的回應：「Valid points.」

　　Valid的意思是「有根據的；令人信服的；合法的；有效的」，例如 valid form（有效的表格）、valid ticket（有效的票）、valid contract（具有法律效力的契約）。

　　Invalid的意思是「無效的」，例如：「A passport that is out of date is invalid.」（護照過期是無效的。）Validate的意思是「使有效；使生效；確認；證實」，這個字常用在系統上的確認，例如員工輸入資料後，需要

主管的validate後才能生效。在電影《紙上城市》中有句台詞：「If we're gonna validate the story, could we get a couple details?」（如果我們要證實這個故事，你可以再講述清楚點嗎？）

　　Validation的意思是「批准；確認」，Validation Test（VT）就是「合格檢查」，它是對硬體所進行的一種測試，目的在於確認硬體是否能正常執行，相關用法及例句請參考以下例句。

1 **Valid** adj. 合理的；令人信服的
They must have a valid reason to do so.
他們必須有合理的理由這樣做。

2 **Valid** adj. 有效的
This license is no longer valid.
這張執照不再有效。

3 **Validate** v. 確認；證實
We have entered the system codes again; can you validate now and confirm everything is fine?
我們已經再次輸入系統代碼，你現在可以驗證並確認一切都可行了嗎？

4 **Validation** n. 批准；確認
The validation report may raise issues that need to be subsequently addressed during project implementation.
這份確認報告可能會提出在專案實施過程中需要被強調的問題。

電影經典名言可以這樣應用

　　在職場上，這句可以應用在雖然表面上看到是如此，但心中仍有遲疑時，就可以這麼說，因為有可能故意製造出來的假象或騙局。

• **Looks can be deceiving.**
眼見不一定為實。
引自《天菜大廚》

Unit 2　掌控會議的進行和發言

　　一個會議有沒有效率、能否得到結論，如何主持及管理會議極其關鍵。有位外籍同事曾傳授我一個訣竅，就是在開會前把討論議題發給幾位與會的重要人物，請他們先表達意見，屆時你便能當場回應他們提出的問題，甚至他們也會幫你回應別人的質疑。

從電影對話中找靈感

引導詢問

▶ Proceed.
你繼續說。 ··· 📹 搖搖欲墜

▶ Moving on.
繼續！ ··· 📹 實習大叔

▶ Your move.
輪你說了。 ··· 📹 驚爆焦點

▶ Keep going.
繼續！ ··· 📹 丹林柯林斯

▶ Focus on positives.
朝好的方面想。 ····································· 📹 靈犬出任務

▶ Where were we?
我們說到哪裡了？ ································· 📹 驚天換日

▶ It's getting close.
愈來愈有樣子了。 ································· 📹 大夢想家

▶ Back to square one.
回到原點。 ┅┅┅┅┅┅┅┅┅┅┅┅┅┅ 📹 我想念我自己

▶ Just jumping in here.
直接說結論吧！ ┅┅┅┅┅┅┅┅┅┅┅ 📹 我想念我自己

▶ Would you skip down?
你可以跳過去嗎？ ┅┅┅┅┅┅┅┅┅┅ 📹 白宮風雲

▶ Do we have a problem?
有人有意見嗎？ ┅┅┅┅┅┅┅┅┅┅┅ 📹 天菜大廚

▶ What do you think so far?
目前為止你有何高見？ ┅┅┅┅┅┅┅┅ 📹 史帝夫賈伯斯

▶ We'll get right to the point.
我們直接切入主題。 ┅┅┅┅┅┅┅┅┅ 📹 白宮風雲

▶ Pick it up from there, please.
請從這兒開始吧！ ┅┅┅┅┅┅┅┅┅┅ 📹 史帝夫賈伯斯

▶ Can we just get pass that?
我們能跳過那些嗎？ ┅┅┅┅┅┅┅┅┅ 📹 機械姬

▶ Spin it out. Whatever it is.
想說什麼，有話直說。 ┅┅┅┅┅┅┅┅ 📹 布魯克林

▶ You need to start from the beginning.
你必須從頭開始說。 ┅┅┅┅┅┅┅┅┅ 📹 人質

▶ Just start back from the beginning.
只好從頭來過。 ┅┅┅┅┅┅┅┅┅┅┅ 📹 白日夢冒險王

▶ The decision's coming down Monday, all right?
星期一來決定，好嗎？ ┅┅┅┅┅┅┅┅ 📹 非禮勿弒

緩和制止

▶ Don't get emotional.
別激動！ ┅┅┅┅┅┅┅┅┅┅┅┅┅┅┅ 📹 空中救援

▶ Hold your horses.
大家冷靜點！ ┅┅┅┅┅┅┅┅┅┅┅┅┅ 📹 搖搖欲墜

▶ Enough of this.
夠了！ .... 🎬 靈犬出任務

▶ Just cool it.
都別說了！ .... 🎬 搖滾女王

▶ That's a bit much.
有點太過了。 .... 🎬 家有兩個爸

▶ Quit being an instigator.
少煽風點火。 .... 🎬 家有兩個爸

▶ You stay out of it.
沒你的事。 .... 🎬 家有兩個爸

▶ Let's keep it tight.
讓我們冷靜一下。 .... 🎬 搖滾女王

▶ You've gone round the bend.
你扯太遠了！ .... 🎬 白宮風雲

▶ We don't need to talk about it anymore.
我們不用再談論這個了。 .... 🎬 凸槌三人行

▶ It's over-discussed at this point.
這事談太久了。 .... 🎬 家有兩個爸

▶ Could you please stop being such a buzzkill?
你們倆可以停止潑冷水嗎？ .... 🎬 大賣空

▶ You guys are getting off the point.
你們離題了。 .... 🎬 實習大叔

▶ We've had this conversation so many times.
這個話題我們談論太多次了。 .... 🎬 愛情失控點

▶ I think we've gotten a little far a field. A little off-topic.
我們離題了，有點離題。 .... 🎬 實習大叔

控制

▶ Boundaries.
注意底線。 .... 🎬 史帝夫賈伯斯

▶ Time's up.
　時間到了。 .... 🎬 心靈捕手

▶ It's getting late.
　現在不早了！ .... 🎬 丹麥女孩

▶ The subject is closed.
　這話題已經結束了。 .... 🎬 非禮勿弒

▶ The conversation is over.
　別說了！ .... 🎬 翻轉幸福

▶ Let's keep it professional.
　讓我們保持專業。 .... 🎬 白宮末日

▶ There's just no time left.
　沒有時間了。 .... 🎬 通靈神探

▶ Let's quit while we're ahead.
　見好就收吧！ .... 🎬 翻轉幸福

▶ I think it's enough now.
　我想適可而止吧！ .... 🎬 45 年

▶ Can we move this along?
　趕快好嗎？ .... 🎬 空中救援

▶ Could you set that aside?
　你可以先擱置那個嗎？ .... 🎬 驚爆焦點

▶ We're on a clock now.
　我們時間不多了。 .... 🎬 驚爆焦點

▶ It's not a high priority.
　這不是優先處理的事。 .... 🎬 白宮風雲

▶ This is no time to discuss this.
　沒時間討論這個。 .... 🎬 無處可逃

▶ There is some material we haven't covered yet.
　有些重點我們還沒談到。 .... 🎬 白宮風雲

▶ Time to shut the engines down for a bit.
　是時候休息一下了。 .... 🎬 實習大叔

歸納總結

▶ That was all.
那就說定了。 ⋯⋯⋯⋯⋯⋯⋯⋯⋯⋯⋯⋯⋯⋯⋯⋯⋯⋯⋯⋯⋯ 🎥 聖母峰

▶ Call to vote.
開始表決吧！ ⋯⋯⋯⋯⋯⋯⋯⋯⋯⋯⋯⋯⋯⋯⋯⋯⋯⋯⋯ 🎥 靈犬出任務

▶ All in favour?
全都贊成？ ⋯⋯⋯⋯⋯⋯⋯⋯⋯⋯⋯⋯⋯⋯⋯⋯⋯⋯⋯⋯ 🎥 靈犬出任務

▶ Let's do side-by-side comparison.
我們來做一下並列比較。 ⋯⋯⋯⋯⋯⋯⋯⋯⋯⋯⋯⋯⋯ 🎥 白宮風雲

▶ I'll take that as an overwhelming yes.
那就是一面倒通過了。 ⋯⋯⋯⋯⋯⋯⋯⋯⋯⋯⋯⋯⋯⋯ 🎥 實習大叔

▶ Let's see if that's at all possible.
讓我們看看有沒有這種可能。 ⋯⋯⋯⋯⋯⋯⋯⋯⋯⋯ 🎥 大夢想家

最容易運用的職場關鍵字　Set

口語中常聽到「We're all set.」意思就是「我們都準備好了」，這裡的set是形容詞，意思是「準備好的」。例如你告訴朋友：「I'll be all set.」（我將會定下來了。）

Set做為動詞的意思是「放；置；調正；校正」，例如電影《非禮勿弒》中有句台詞：「Are you setting in okay?」（你安置得還好嗎？）Set做為名詞的意思是「一盤比賽；樂團」，網球術語的set point就是「盤末點」。在電影《搖滾女王》中有句台詞：「Great set.」意思是很好的樂團，衍生之意為「表演得不錯」。

Set up的意思是「使（設備、機器）準備就序；建立或開創某事物」，例如老闆說：「晚上的演講，你提前30分鐘到現場set up。」電影《驚爆焦點》中有句台詞：「It's set up for next week.」（就訂下周。）

Setting的意思是「安裝；裝置；設定」，可以用在書或影片中情節發

生的地點或時間。還有一個慣用語叫「set up to the plate」，當棒球員要打擊時必須先站上本壘板（plate），set up to the plate意味著要開始打擊了，衍生之意為「開始行動」。其他和set的相關用法請參閱以下例句。

1 Set v. 設定
I think we should set minimum subscription amount for the new product.
我想我們應該為新產品設定最低購買金額。

2 Set up ph. 使（設備、機器）準備就序
How long will it take to set up the projector?
把投影機準備好需要多長時間？

3 Set up ph. 建立；建造
That is the way the system is set up.
這個體系就是這樣運作的。

4 Set up to the plate ph. 開始行動
You should set up to the plate.
你該行動起來了。

電影經典名言可以這樣應用

　　這句話出現在主角對朋友說：「怎麼這麼早」，朋友如此回覆，在電影中也有這麼說：「Early bird gets the free donuts and coffee.」在職場上，若看到同事在某個場合很早到，也可以這麼說。

- **The early bird catches the worm.**
早起的鳥兒有蟲吃。　　　　　　　　　　　　　　　引自《心靈大道》

Unit 3 適時表達看法的適用對話

參加會議一定要適度表達意見，若真的沒什麼意見，至少學會正面、負面或中性的簡單回應，讓別人知道你所代表部門的立場。

簡短回應的各種說法

正面回應			
Positive.	確定。	Absolutely right.	完全正確。
That's fair.	說得沒錯。	Fair enough.	不錯。
Fair point	說得有道理。	That's right.	沒錯。
Damn straight.	一點也沒錯。	Quite possibly.	很有可能。
No question.	毫無疑問。	Pretty trustworthy.	應該信得過。
Insanely great.	真是不錯。	That's good.	那很好。
Kinda brilliant.	絕妙主意。	It's for real.	是真的。
That's good point.	這說法有道理。	Count on it.	那是一定的。
Couldn't agree more.	再同意不過了。	It's good a idea.	好主意。
Make perfect sense.	十分合理。	It's worth a try.	值得一試。
That's very accurate.	非常正確。	More than likely.	很有可能。
That's really cool.	這個想法很好。	That's very observant.	很有觀察力。

That's exactly right.	完全正確。	That's a good one.	不錯的想法。
I'm sure it is.	我相信是。	No question about it.	絕對沒錯。
These should be fine.	這些應該沒問題。	It's all very logical.	這是非常符合邏輯。
That sounds good news.	那真是好消息。	That would be helpful.	那會有幫助。

負面回應

Nonsense.	胡說。	No guarantees.	沒有保證。
Not directly.	沒有直接相關。	It's unethical.	這不道德。
Not necessarily.	那不一定。	Sounds thin.	聽起來沒什麼料。
That's debatable.	那可不一定。	Not a chance.	門都沒有。
It doesn't matter.	那不重要。	It's an old trick.	這是老梗。
Never gonna happen.	不可能。	There's no way.	不可能。
That's not practical.	這不實用。	That's not necessary.	沒必要。
Make no promises.	不保證。	Quite the contrary.	恰好相反。
There are variables.	會有變數。	It's not a necessity.	沒有必要。
No, it's not that.	不，不是那樣的。	That wouldn't appropriate.	那麼做並不恰當。
It's not like that.	不是那樣。	It's nothing like that.	不是那樣。
Doesn't look like that.	看起來不像是。	Doesn't look like much.	看起來不怎麼樣。
I'm not so sure.	不很確定。	No chance of that.	機會不太大。
That's not gonna happen.	那個辦不到。	This is completely bullshit.	這完全是胡說八道。

續下頁 >

That doesn't prove anything.	那不能證明什麼。	That won't be necessary.	沒有那個必要。
Sounds low to me.	我覺得太少了。	This is not working.	這樣不行。
Not easy thing to do.	不容易辦到。	It doesn't hold up.	這不成立。
It doesn't work like that.	這樣行不通。	Not the perfect metaphor.	不是很好的比喻。
There's nothing we can do.	我們也無能為力。	We shouldn't be doing this.	我們不應該這麼做。
It's more complicated than that.	沒那麼簡單。	I don't see the connection.	這完全無關。
It doesn't look that way.	看起來不是那樣。	It doesn't feel that way.	感覺不是這樣。

中性回應

Couldn't hurt.	可以試試。	I suppose.	應該可以。
It depends.	看情況。	Cautious optimism.	審慎樂觀。
Hard to say.	說不準。	Maybe they are.	也許是真的。
Up to a point.	某程度上是。	It's a possibility.	有這種可能。
Looks like it.	看起來是。	Not so much.	不算是。
I have no argument.	我毫無異議。	I wouldn't mind it.	我不介意。
There may be a market.	也許會有市場。	It's not my judgement.	我無法判斷。
That ought to count for something.	應該有用吧！	There is no good or bad here.	沒什麼對錯。

從電影對話中找靈感

▶ You'd be very convincing.
  你會很有說服力。⋯⋯⋯⋯⋯⋯⋯⋯⋯⋯⋯⋯⋯⋯⋯ 📹◀ 丹麥女孩

▶ It looks kind of fancy.
  看起來不錯。⋯⋯⋯⋯⋯⋯⋯⋯⋯⋯⋯⋯⋯⋯⋯⋯⋯ 📹◀ 凸槌三人行

▶ It's pretty clear pattern.
  這是很明顯的模式。⋯⋯⋯⋯⋯⋯⋯⋯⋯⋯⋯⋯⋯⋯⋯ 📹◀ 驚爆焦點

▶ Right on that button.
  說得很準確。⋯⋯⋯⋯⋯⋯⋯⋯⋯⋯⋯⋯⋯⋯⋯⋯⋯ 📹◀ 心靈捕手

▶ It's a well-thought out concept.
  一切都考慮得很周全。⋯⋯⋯⋯⋯⋯⋯⋯⋯⋯⋯⋯⋯⋯ 📹◀ 愛情失控點

▶ That's a canny observation.
  觀察力還真入微。⋯⋯⋯⋯⋯⋯⋯⋯⋯⋯⋯⋯⋯⋯⋯⋯ 📹◀ 大夢想家

▶ I don't doubt it a second.
  那是當然了。⋯⋯⋯⋯⋯⋯⋯⋯⋯⋯⋯⋯⋯⋯⋯⋯⋯ 📹◀ 45 年

▶ I trust you blindly.
  我無條件相信你。⋯⋯⋯⋯⋯⋯⋯⋯⋯⋯⋯⋯⋯⋯⋯⋯ 📹◀ 拍賣家

▶ It's not totally off the wall.
  也不是毫無根據。⋯⋯⋯⋯⋯⋯⋯⋯⋯⋯⋯⋯⋯⋯⋯⋯ 📹◀ 愛情失控點

▶ That's hardly surprising.
  一點都不意外。⋯⋯⋯⋯⋯⋯⋯⋯⋯⋯⋯⋯⋯⋯⋯⋯⋯ 📹◀ 大夢想家

▶ But it's not in cement.
  但事情還沒塵埃落定。⋯⋯⋯⋯⋯⋯⋯⋯⋯⋯⋯⋯⋯⋯ 📹◀ 白宮風雲

▶ I don't think that big impact.
  我認為並沒有多大影響。⋯⋯⋯⋯⋯⋯⋯⋯⋯⋯⋯⋯⋯ 📹◀ 驚爆焦點

▶ So it was the other way around.
  所以事實正好相反。⋯⋯⋯⋯⋯⋯⋯⋯⋯⋯⋯⋯⋯⋯⋯ 📹◀ 史帝夫賈伯斯

▶ But to be completely frank, it wasn't enough.
  但是坦白說，那完全不夠。⋯⋯⋯⋯⋯⋯⋯⋯⋯⋯⋯ 📹◀ 驚爆焦點

▶ It's not unusual in cases like that.
這情況倒是很常見。 ……………………………………………… 📹 心靈大道

▶ There is no way that makes sense.
這顯然沒道理啊！ …………………………………………………… 📹 大賣空

▶ Not sure it works like that.
不一定是這樣。 ……………………………………………………… 📹 45 年

▶ That doesn't make any sense at all.
這一點道理都沒有。 ………………………………………………… 📹 我想念我自己

▶ It's more complicated than you think.
這比你想的還複雜。 ………………………………………………… 📹 驚天換日

▶ I think it's a big mistake. Apart from time and resources.
我覺得這是天大的錯誤，不光是浪費的時間和資源。 ……… 📹 通靈神探

▶ That's not how things work.
事情不是這樣運作的。 ……………………………………………… 📹 拍賣家

當你要強調說明時，也可用如下的說法：

1	To reiterate…… 再次重申……
2	As I recall. 我記得。
3	Having said that. 話說回來。
4	I'll be honest. 老實說。
5	Given the circumstances. 基於這種情況。
6	To put it simply. 簡單地說。
7	Let me rephrase that. 我換個說法。
8	I need to make this clear. 我得聲明一下。
9	Let me put it this/another way. 讓我這麼說吧！
10	I wanna make this clear to everybody. 我要很清楚的說。

當你沒跟上討論時，也可用如下的說法：

1	I don't get it. 我不明白。
2	I'm not getting that. 我沒聽懂。
3	I'm completely lost. 我完全聽不明白。
4	I'm not following this. 我沒聽明白。
5	I have absolutely no idea. 我一點頭緒也沒有。
6	I don't know the difference. 我不知道兩者的差別。

最容易運用的職場關鍵字　Like

　　Like 做為介系詞的意思是「像；如」，例如電影《非禮勿弒》中有句台詞：「You are out like a light.」（你睡著了。）Like 和 look, sound 及 seem 經常一起使用，例如 look like, sound like, seem like，但都可以翻譯成「像要；好像是」，例如：「Look like you just learned.」（好像是你才剛知道。）

　　Like 做為動詞意思是「喜歡」，例如「I like to travel light.」（我喜歡輕裝旅行。）做為形容詞的意思是「相像的」，例如說：「Your boy is exactly like you.」（你兒子很像你。）做為連接詞的意思是「如同；好像」，例如 Like you said......（如你所言……）。

　　由 like 所衍生出來的字有 likely（大概；很可能的），例如 very likely（非常有可能的）及 most likely（最有可能的），其反義字為 unlikely（難以相信的；不大可能發生的）。其他和 like 的相關用法請參閱以下例句。

1 Like v. 喜歡；欣賞
I like the motto of the company.
我欣賞公司的座右銘。

2 Like `prep.` 像；如

I want to see a comprehensive list. Not a high level one like that.

我希望看到一個完整的列表，不是像高階那樣。

---

3 Look like `ph.` 像要；好像是

Look like we're in business.

看起來我們可以營業了。

---

4 Likely `adj.` 大概；很可能的

It's likely that she'll arrive before eleven.

她大概在十一點前會到。

---

5 Unlikely `adj.` 難以相信的；不大可能發生的

She gave me an unlikely explanation for being late.

她給了我難以令人信服的遲到說明。

電影經典名言可以這樣應用

這可以運用在強調動腦比動力更重要的狀況中。

- **The pen is mightier than sword.**
  文攻勝過武略。   引自《白宮末日》

Unit 4　會議提問的慣常用語

　　開會除了積極回應外，若想讓自己在開會時表現得更突出，就要學會問問題。

不同反問的各種說法

英文	中譯	英文	中譯
二字問句			
Which way?	哪方面？	Like what?	比如說？
三字問句			
On what grounds?	以什麼理由？	Is that acceptable?	這樣可以接受嗎？
Don't you think?	你不認為？	This isn't fake?	這不是合成的吧？
What's the point?	重點為何？	What'd you find?	你發現什麼？
Is that possible?	這可能嗎？	Is that problem?	有問題嗎？
Any particular reason?	有具體原因嗎？	Cite your source?	有何根據？
四字問句			
What's the difference?	有差別嗎？	What's your point?	你想說什麼？
Where is its heart?	它的意義在哪？	What do you say?	你說怎麼樣？
What does that matter?	那重要嗎？	Does it really matter?	這真重要嗎？
Would it be possible?	這可能嗎？	Is that a problem?	有問題嗎？

續下頁 >

英文	中譯	英文	中譯
What do we get?	我們有什麼好處？	Are you for real?	你不是在說笑吧？
That's what you're saying?	那就是你的意思嗎？	Does that sound good?	可行嗎？
Why didn't anyone listen?	怎麼沒人願意聽我說？	How is that possible?	怎麼可能？
Did I forget any?	我有說漏嗎？	What's supposed to mean?	那是什麼意思？
Would it be possible?	有可能嗎？	Whose idea was that?	誰的主意？
How'd you find out?	你怎麼知道的？	Is that really possible?	真的可能嗎？
How can it hurt?	有什麼壞處？	What do you got?	你有什麼點子？
Why are we hesitating?	我們為什麼要遲疑？	How they go out?	結果如何？
That was one-off?	那是一次性的嗎？	Is that a concern?	這會有問題嗎？
The pros and cons?	利弊如何？	We think it's legal?	這合法嗎？
How bad is this?	情況有多嚴重？	What's the plan?	我們怎麼做？
Don't you get it?	你不明白嗎？	Does this look familiar?	這情況似曾相似嗎？
五字問句			
Are you following of this?	你都聽得懂吧？	How would you do that?	你要怎麼處理？
Are you sure about that?	你確定嗎？	You know what I mean?	知道我的意思嗎？
Can you go into details?	能不能說詳細一點？	You see what I'm saying?	你明白我的意思了吧？

英文	中譯	英文	中譯
How long can that last?	能撐多久？	What makes you so sure?	你為什麼那麼確定？
What are the real projections?	真實的預測是多少？	Am I reading this right?	我沒看錯吧？
Why are you defending her?	你為什麼要幫她說話？	You follow what I'm saying.	你明白我說的意思嗎？
What's in it for me?	這對我有什麼好處？	You still don't get it?	你還是不明白嗎？
Anything else you can recall?	你能想起任何事嗎？	Can you see that working?	你覺得行得通嗎？
You guys didn't see it?	你們不明白嗎？	How long would it take?	需要多久？
How much will it cost?	要花多少錢？	How is that still legal?	那怎麼是合法的？
What am I missing here?	我漏掉什麼？	How did you do that?	你怎麼辦到的？
How's that for a compromise?	這折衷的辦法怎麼樣？	What's the policy on that?	規定是什麼？
六字問句			
What did you have in mind?	你有什麼計畫？	Who thinks of things like that?	誰會想到這些？
Is that really what you think?	你真的這麼想？	Did you follow up on that?	你有後續追蹤嗎？
Why didn't we get it sooner?	為什麼我們沒有早點行動？	You know what it stood for?	你知道它代表什麼嗎？
Is that your angle you're making?	那就是你的立場？	I have your word on that?	你願意保證嗎？

英文	中譯	英文	中譯
Where are you going with this?	你的重點到底是什麼？	What is there to think about?	還有什麼好想的？
What exactly is it you want?	你到底想幹嘛？	Is that too much to ask?	這要求過分嗎？
So now what do we do?	那我們現在怎麼辦？	Would you mind expanding on that?	請你再說詳細點好嗎？

從電影對話中找靈感

▶ Where'd you come up with that idea?
你是怎麼想到的？ ……………………………………… 🎥 天菜大廚

▶ How long does that typically take?
那一般需要多長時間？ …………………………………… 🎥 驚爆焦點

▶ How fast could you do something like that?
你能多快搞定那種事？ …………………………………… 🎥 空中救援

▶ How do you propose we do that?
你打算怎麼做？ …………………………………………… 🎥 白宮末日

▶ What is your take on the situation?
你對這情勢的看法如何？ ………………………………… 🎥 白宮風雲

▶ Isn't that the way it's supposed to go?
事情不是應該這樣發展嗎？ ……………………………… 🎥 驚天換日

▶ Do you have any proof of that?
你能拿出什麼證據嗎？ …………………………………… 🎥 驚爆焦點

▶ Does that number sound right to you?
你覺得這數字準確嗎？ …………………………………… 🎥 驚爆焦點

▶ You're completely sure of the math?
你計算沒問題吧？ ………………………………………… 🎥 大賣空

▶ Did you manage to understand some of it?
你有稍微看懂嗎？ ·· 📹◀ 拍賣家

▶ Would you unpack that for me?
你能詳細說清楚嗎？ ·· 📹◀ 我想念我自己

▶ How about a final push?
再試最後一次吧？ ·· 📹◀ 靈犬出任務

▶ Is end of today too ambitious?
設定今天完成會不會期望太高了？ ···················· 📹◀ 非禮勿弒

「等一下！」的各種說法

1	Wait a minute.
2	Just a moment.
3	Hold on a minute.
4	Hang on.
5	Stop for a second.
6	Give me one second.
7	Just give it a second.
8	Let's hold it.
9	Wait, hold on a second.

最容易運用的職場關鍵字　Source

　　Source 做為名詞的意思是「來源；根源；出處」，在做PPT簡報資料時，若引用別人的資料，就必須在下方註明 data source（資料來源）。

　　Resource 的意思是「資源；財力；物力」，像是 natural resource（天然資源）及 human resource（人力資源），例如：「His team is very tight in resources.」（他的團隊人力非常吃緊。）在電影《驚爆焦點》中有句台詞：「Do you think your paper has resources to take that on?」（你覺得你們報社有實力去挑戰它嗎？）

　　Outsource 的意思是「外包；外購」，有些工作不是公司擅長或不是長期業務，為了節省成本，公司會把工作 outsource 給其他公司做。近年來，這種趨勢愈來愈明顯，例如電腦部門、作業部門、電話中心，甚至連財務會計，都可以 outsource 到中國大陸、印度、馬來西亞等具備成本優勢且沒有語言障礙的國家。其他和 source 相關的用法請參閱以下例句。

1 Resource n. 資源；人力

We are experiencing resource shortage now. I'll arrange secondee arrangement to help.

我們現在遇到人力短缺。我會安排借調人員來協助。

2 Outsource v. 外包

If you can't do it, I'll have to outsource.

如果你做不了，我只好外包了。

Unit 5 意見不合的表達用語

　　每個部門都會有本位主義，加上工作永遠做不完，多一事不如少一事，基於上述原因，開會出現互推工作、意見不同及衝突場面在所難免。

從電影對話中找靈感

　　　　　　　　　　跟「質疑」有關的語句

▶ Why bother?
　何必多此一舉？ .... 🎥 史帝夫賈伯斯

▶ Didn't or couldn't?
　是不想還是不能？ .... 🎥 天菜大廚

▶ Don't be offended.
　不要防衛心那麼重。 .... 🎥 搖滾女王

▶ Where is its reality?
　真實性在哪？ .... 🎥 大夢想家

▶ You are blind to it.
　你是視而不見。 .... 🎥 全面進化

▶ But what if it isn't?
　但如果不是？ .... 🎥 史帝夫賈伯斯

▶ Was it worth the risk?
　值得冒這個險嗎？ .... 🎥 愛情失控點

▶ That is out of line.
　這就有失公道了。 .... 🎥 白宮風雲

▶ Don't be so close-minded.
別這麼思想封閉。 ………………………………… 🎥◀ 驚天換日

▶ It isn't a big deal.
這沒什麼大不了。 ………………………………… 🎥◀ 白宮風雲

▶ I'm not seeing your point.
不明白你想表達什麼。 …………………………… 🎥◀ 丹林柯林斯

▶ You wanna make an exception?
你想破例？ ……………………………………… 🎥◀ 驚天換日

▶ Just answer the question, will you?
你能不能正面回答問題？ ……………………… 🎥◀ 驚爆焦點

▶ Is that what's agenda today?
那是今天的議題嗎？ …………………………… 🎥◀ 弒訊

▶ You don't have to do this.
你沒必要這麼做。 ……………………………… 🎥◀ 人質

▶ You don't have to get too graphic.
你不用太繪聲繪影。 …………………………… 🎥◀ 愛情失控點

▶ Why hasn't this been brought up?
為何這問題之前沒有提出來？ ………………… 🎥◀ 白宮風雲

▶ You missed a few steps in between.
你中間漏了幾個步驟。 ………………………… 🎥◀ 與外婆同行

▶ I'm not sure what you're telling me.
我不確定你想表達什麼。 ……………………… 🎥◀ 布魯克林

▶ You'd like to go around in circles.
你想要繞圈子。 ………………………………… 🎥◀ 驚天換日

▶ I don't even know what language you're speaking right now.
我根本不知道你現在在講什麼火星話。 ……… 🎥◀ 白日夢冒險王

跟「不滿」有關的語句

▶ We're finished here.
沒什麼好談的。 ⋯⋯⋯⋯⋯⋯⋯⋯⋯⋯⋯⋯⋯⋯⋯ 聖母峰

▶ You're too paranoid.
你太偏執了。 ⋯⋯⋯⋯⋯⋯⋯⋯⋯⋯⋯⋯⋯⋯⋯ 愛情失控點

▶ You are very much mistaken.
你大錯特錯了。 ⋯⋯⋯⋯⋯⋯⋯⋯⋯⋯⋯⋯⋯⋯⋯ 偷書賊

▶ You're preaching to the choir.
你別費唇舌了。 ⋯⋯⋯⋯⋯⋯⋯⋯⋯⋯⋯⋯⋯⋯⋯ 空中救援

▶ Don't tap dance with me.
別跟我兜圈子。 ⋯⋯⋯⋯⋯⋯⋯⋯⋯⋯⋯⋯⋯⋯⋯ 愛情失控點

▶ You just tricked me a little.
你在耍我。 ⋯⋯⋯⋯⋯⋯⋯⋯⋯⋯⋯⋯⋯⋯⋯⋯ 史帝夫賈伯斯

▶ Why don't you leave people alone?
你不能放過別人嗎？ ⋯⋯⋯⋯⋯⋯⋯⋯⋯⋯⋯⋯⋯ 驚天換日

▶ You just drop a grenade in my lap.
你把麻煩丟給我了。 ⋯⋯⋯⋯⋯⋯⋯⋯⋯⋯⋯⋯⋯ 搖搖欲墜

▶ You know that sounds pretty ridiculous.
你知道這聽起來很荒謬。 ⋯⋯⋯⋯⋯⋯⋯⋯⋯⋯⋯ 白宮風雲

▶ Do you want to try being reasonable?
你能試著講點道理嗎？ ⋯⋯⋯⋯⋯⋯⋯⋯⋯⋯⋯ 史帝夫賈伯斯

▶ Obviously they're not big on logic.
顯然邏輯不通。 ⋯⋯⋯⋯⋯⋯⋯⋯⋯⋯⋯⋯⋯⋯⋯ 全面進化

▶ You're blowing this all out of the proportion.
你這是在小題大做。 ⋯⋯⋯⋯⋯⋯⋯⋯⋯⋯⋯⋯ 時空永恆的愛戀

▶ Do you really want to challenge me in public?
你真的要在公開場合挑戰我嗎？ ⋯⋯⋯⋯⋯⋯⋯⋯ 凸槌三人行

▶ You talk a big game but never do anything about it.
你很會畫大餅但從來不做。 ·········· 🎥 實習大叔

▶ You sure you have really got that theory down.
你確定那理論搞清楚了。 ·········· 🎥 愛情失控點

▶ You can't justify it with all this bullshit.
你不能拿這些扯淡的理由來找藉口。 ·········· 🎥 愛情失控點

▶ That is your opinion. You just happen to be wrong.
那是你的看法，剛好你錯了。 ·········· 🎥 全面進化

▶ Are you seriously talking about this right now?
你真的要現在來談論此事嗎？ ·········· 🎥 翻轉幸福

▶ Things don't become so because you say so.
不是你說什麼就是什麼。 ·········· 🎥 史帝夫賈伯斯

跟「反擊」有關的語句

▶ You're stigmatizing.
你這是血口噴人。 ·········· 🎥 史帝夫賈伯斯

▶ You're killing me.
你真狠。 ·········· 🎥 派特的幸福劇本

▶ That is outrageous.
這太過分了。 ·········· 🎥 丹麥女孩

▶ How dare you?
你怎麼可以？ ·········· 🎥 實習大叔

▶ You're driving me crazy.
你快把我逼瘋了。 ·········· 🎥 大賣空

▶ This is highly distressing.
你這太過分了。 ·········· 🎥 大賣空

▶ Stop being an asshole.
別那麼混蛋。 ·········· 🎥 紙上城市

▶ I knew men like you.
我看透你這種人。 ··· 🎥 空中救援

▶ You better watch yourself.
你最好注意一點。 ··· 🎥 與外婆同行

▶ Please, don't patronize me.
拜託，別給我來這套。 ··· 🎥 大賣空

▶ Why are you so bossy?
你幹嘛那麼盛氣凌人？ ··· 🎥 與外婆同行

▶ You don't get to say that.
你沒資格說這話。 ··· 🎥 搖搖欲墜

▶ You get out of my sight.
離開我的視線／滾開。 ··· 🎥 驚天換日

▶ Where do you get off?
你是不是有毛病？ ··· 🎥 史帝夫賈伯斯

▶ I don't appreciate your tone of voice.
我不喜歡你說話的方式。 ··· 🎥 當辣妹來敲門

▶ You don't talk to me like that in front of my men.
不要在我的人面前那樣對我講話。 ··· 🎥 白宮末日

▶ Why are you giving me such a hard time?
你為什麼要和我過不去？ ··· 🎥 派特的幸福劇本

▶ If you have a problem with me, say it to my face.
對我有意見就當面說。 ··· 🎥 空中救援

▶ Do not throw our inception agreement in my face.
別給我扯官腔。 ··· 🎥 大賣空

最容易運用的職場關鍵字　Drop

在社交英文中，常會對別人說：「如果你有機會到我們公司附近，請
drop by me（順便來拜訪我），我可以請你喝咖啡。」

Drop 做為動詞的意思是「丟下；扔下；下降；下車」，例如你對朋
友說：「Please drop me in front of the company.」（請讓我在公司門口
下車。）「We dropped the ball.」表面上的意思是把球丟下，衍生之意是
「我們這次出了差錯」。

Drop 做為名詞的意思是「落下；下降」，例如老闆說：「The drop in
sales this month is unacceptable.」（這個月業績下滑是無法接受的。）

和 drop 相關的片語，除了 drop by 外，最常見的是 drop off（減少；
衰落）、drop sb. a line（給某人寫信），相關用法請參閱以下例句。

---

1 Drop v. 丟棄；省略

That's why I'm trying to drop it.
所以我才不想提這事了。

---

2 Drop n. 落下；下降

The drop in oil price was quite unexpected.
油價下跌是完全沒有料到的。

---

3 Drop by ph. 順便拜訪

Would you drop by when you are in Taipei?
當你來台北時就來找我好嗎？

---

4 Drop off ph. 減少；衰落

Product A registered good momentum in May which offset the
drop off in product B income.
產品A在五月顯示有好的動能，那抵消了產品B收入的下降。

---

5 Drop sb. a line ph. 給某人寫信

Drop me a line when you get to Singapore.
當你到了新加坡，寫封信給我。

Unit 6　澄清誤會的說法

　　在開會討論過程中，有時會無心觸怒同事，此時要立即補救，以免產生誤會。

從電影對話中找靈感

▶ No offense.
無意冒犯。 ···························· 🎥 愛睡在一起

▶ Nothing personal.
不是針對你個人。 ···················· 🎥 凸槌三人行

▶ Just some clarity.
只想把話說清楚。 ···················· 🎥 全面進化

▶ I didn't say that.
我沒有這麼說。 ······················ 🎥 我想念我自己

▶ I never said that.
我從沒說過。 ························ 🎥 大賣空

▶ It wasn't personal.
不是針對個人。 ······················ 🎥 丹麥女孩

▶ Don't take it personally.
不是針對你。 ························ 🎥 愛情失控點

▶ Don't get me wrong.
別誤會！ ·························· 🎥 高年級實習生

▶ I think you're misunderstanding.
我想你誤會了。 ······················ 🎥 家有兩個爸

▶ I make no judgements.
我不是在批評人。 ···················· 🎥 白宮風雲

▶ I didn't mean you.
我不是指你。 ··· 📹 心靈捕手

▶ I'm doing my job.
我只是在做本份的工作。 ····································· 📹 靈犬出任務

▶ Sorry, that's too much.
抱歉，話有點重了！ ··· 📹 搖搖欲墜

▶ I'm not saying that.
我沒有那麼說。 ··· 📹 心靈捕手

▶ That really wasn't my business.
那真的不關我的事。 ··· 📹 史帝夫賈伯斯

▶ Must have been my mistake.
那麼是我搞錯了。 ··· 📹 家有兩個爸

▶ That's not what I meant.
我不是那個意思。 ··· 📹 當辣妹來敲門

▶ That's not what I said.
我不是這麼說的。 ··· 📹 通靈神探

▶ I'm sorry to be blunt.
抱歉，我口無遮攔。 ··· 📹 史帝夫賈伯斯

▶ Don't take this the wrong way.
別誤會！ ··· 📹 心靈捕手

▶ That's not remotely what I said.
我根本沒這麼說。 ··· 📹 史帝夫賈伯斯

▶ This is not what you think.
不是你想的那樣。 ··· 📹 驚天換日

▶ I didn't mean it like that.
我不是那個意思。 ··· 📹 加州大地震

▶ How am I supposed to do that?
我有什麼辦法啊？ ··· 📹 空中救援

▶ I'm sorry I raised my voice.
抱歉，我說話大聲了。 ····································· 📹 凸槌三人行

▶ We're sorry for the mix-up.
抱歉，我們搞錯了。⋯⋯⋯⋯⋯⋯⋯⋯⋯⋯⋯⋯⋯⋯⋯⋯ 🎥◀ 謎樣的雙眼

▶ Sorry, I'm not paying attention.
抱歉，我剛剛沒注意到。⋯⋯⋯⋯⋯⋯⋯⋯⋯⋯⋯⋯⋯⋯ 🎥◀ 心靈大道

▶ I'm not explaining myself very well.
我表達得不夠好。⋯⋯⋯⋯⋯⋯⋯⋯⋯⋯⋯⋯⋯⋯⋯⋯⋯ 🎥◀ 拍賣家

▶ This wasn't an easy decision for me.
我也不願意這樣。⋯⋯⋯⋯⋯⋯⋯⋯⋯⋯⋯⋯⋯⋯⋯⋯⋯ 🎥◀ 大夢想家

▶ I'm not telling you, I am asking.
我不是在吩咐你，是詢問。⋯⋯⋯⋯⋯⋯⋯⋯⋯⋯⋯⋯⋯ 🎥◀ 聖母峰

▶ I don't want to get sideways with you.
我不想和你爭辯。⋯⋯⋯⋯⋯⋯⋯⋯⋯⋯⋯⋯⋯⋯⋯⋯⋯ 🎥◀ 實習大叔

▶ But with all due respect, that actually wasn't my fault.
我無意冒犯，但那真的不是我的錯。⋯⋯⋯⋯⋯⋯⋯⋯⋯ 🎥◀ 翻轉幸福

換種說法也可通

中譯	常用說法	另類說法
馬上過去。	I'll be right there.	In a minute.《白宮風雲》
開工吧！	Get to work.	Enter the dragon.《搖搖欲墜》
接受它！	Accept it.	Jack it up.《搖搖欲墜》
我完全同意。	I totally agree.	I agree with that completely.《愛情失控點》

最容易運用的職場關鍵字 | Mean

Mean 做為動詞最常解釋為「意思是；意味著」，當你不理解別人的話，就會問：「What do you mean?」（你的意思是什麼？）當你表達對某件事情的看法，可能會說：「It has to mean something.」（肯定意味著些什麼）或「It doesn't mean anything.」（沒什麼特別意義）。在電影《搖滾女王》中有句台詞：「It really means a lot to me that you came.」（你能來真的對我意義重大。）

Mean 還有一個常用的意思是「打算；故意」，例如：「I mean to tell you.」（我本來要告訴你。）Mean it 的意思是「真心的：故意的」，在職場中也經常使用，例如你不是隨便說說或開玩笑，就可以說：「I mean it.」（我是認真的。）或是你幫同事圓場時可以說：「He didn't mean it.」（他不是存心的。）在電影《白宮末日》中有句台詞：「Show them we mean business.」（讓他們知道我們是玩真的。）

Mean 做為形容詞多半是負面的意思，例如「苛薄的；凶惡的；小氣的；卑鄙的」，在職場上有時會聽到別人說：「這個人很mean。」還有「That was a mean trick.」（那是一個卑鄙的詭計。）其他和mean相關的用法請參閱以下例句。

1 **Mean** v. 意思是；意指
We don't mean to be disrespectful.
我們不是有意冒犯你。

2 **Be meant to** v. 必須要；註定要
Some things just aren't meant to be.
有些事情注定無法成真。

3 **By means of** ph. 用；藉著
He solved the problem by means of simple equations.
他利用簡單的方程式解決了這問題。

4 **By all means** ph. 盡一切辦法；務必；一定
We have to finish our task by all means.
我們必須竭力完成任務。

Unit 7　適時表達意見增加參與感

　　好的回應及詢問就能參與會議到一定程度，但最重要的還是能表達好的觀點及意見。

從電影對話中找靈感

▶ It's bargaining chip.
這是談判籌碼。⋯⋯⋯⋯⋯⋯⋯⋯⋯⋯⋯⋯⋯⋯⋯⋯🎥◀ 拍賣家

▶ It's pretty straight forward.
簡單易行。⋯⋯⋯⋯⋯⋯⋯⋯⋯⋯⋯⋯⋯⋯⋯⋯⋯🎥◀ 驚爆焦點

▶ That's how it works.
這就是規則。⋯⋯⋯⋯⋯⋯⋯⋯⋯⋯⋯⋯⋯⋯⋯⋯🎥◀ 史帝夫賈伯斯

▶ That would be counterproductive.
那樣只會適得其反。⋯⋯⋯⋯⋯⋯⋯⋯⋯⋯⋯⋯⋯🎥◀ 我想念我自己

▶ It's a closed loop.
是個死胡同。⋯⋯⋯⋯⋯⋯⋯⋯⋯⋯⋯⋯⋯⋯⋯⋯🎥◀ 機械姬

▶ I see no other way.
別無出路。⋯⋯⋯⋯⋯⋯⋯⋯⋯⋯⋯⋯⋯⋯⋯⋯⋯🎥◀ 愛情失控點

▶ That's my two cents.
這是我的拙見。⋯⋯⋯⋯⋯⋯⋯⋯⋯⋯⋯⋯⋯⋯⋯🎥◀ 大賣空

▶ This is the consistency.
這是共同點。⋯⋯⋯⋯⋯⋯⋯⋯⋯⋯⋯⋯⋯⋯⋯⋯🎥◀ 通靈神探

▶ There's no understudy.
沒有後路了。⋯⋯⋯⋯⋯⋯⋯⋯⋯⋯⋯⋯⋯⋯⋯⋯🎥◀ 搖滾女王

▶ This shouldn't take a second.
花不了多少時間。⋯⋯⋯⋯⋯⋯⋯⋯⋯⋯⋯⋯⋯⋯🎥◀ 偷書賊

▶ It's too soon to tell.
現在還言之過早。 ·· 拍賣家

▶ That's the way it is.
這是大勢所趨。 ·· 凸槌三人行

▶ It's a conflict of interest.
這是有利益衝突的。 ·· 搖搖欲墜

▶ This is when mistakes occur.
這種時候就會犯錯。 ·· 拍賣家

▶ I guess a little of both.
兩者都有一點吧！ ·· 愛情沒有終點

▶ That's the hell of a precedent.
這可是前所未有啊！ ·· 驚爆焦點

▶ Maybe this will be a big break.
或許這會是個突破。 ·· 我想念我自己

▶ Simply the way the world works.
世界就是這麼運轉。 ·· 大賣空

▶ It's an once-in-a-lifetime deal.
這是千載難逢的好機會。 ·· 大賣空

▶ That's gonna be the real breakthrough.
這將會有真正的突破。 ·· 機械姬

▶ It makes no difference.
這沒有什麼區別。 ·· 拍賣家

▶ This happens sometimes in business.
生意上有時會發生這種事。 ·· 翻轉幸福

▶ This deal is getting close to finish the line.
這交易已經穩操勝算了。 ·· 凸槌三人行

▶ It's not a matter of "if" but "when".
只是早晚的問題。 ·· 愛情沒有終點

▶ I think it's way too early to jump into conclusions.
我覺得現在下結論還太早。 ⋯⋯⋯⋯⋯⋯⋯⋯⋯⋯⋯⋯⋯⋯⋯ 🎥◀ 我想念我自己

▶ Sounds like it was more than that.
聽起來可不只如此。 ⋯⋯⋯⋯⋯⋯⋯⋯⋯⋯⋯⋯⋯⋯⋯⋯⋯⋯⋯ 🎥◀ 時空永恆的愛戀

▶ I thought that this is the best option available.
我覺得這是所能做的最佳選擇。 ⋯⋯⋯⋯⋯⋯⋯⋯⋯⋯⋯⋯⋯⋯ 🎥◀ 無處可逃

▶ Those figures require interpretation.
不能光看表面數目。 ⋯⋯⋯⋯⋯⋯⋯⋯⋯⋯⋯⋯⋯⋯⋯⋯⋯⋯⋯⋯ 🎥◀ 拍賣家

換種說法也可通

中譯	常用說法	另類說法
這是一個極好的主意。	This is a great idea.	This is a tremendous idea.《紙上城市》
全是胡說八道。	It's all bullshit.	It's a total crack of shit.《驚天換日》
不算難。	It's easy.	There's nothing to it.《愛情沒有終點》
這我沒意見。	I'm fine with it.	I don't have a problem with that.《白宮末日》

最容易運用的職場關鍵字 | **Way**

　　當你開會遲到，別人打電話問你在哪裡？你就可以簡單地回答：「I'm on the way.」（我正在路上。）這裡的 Way 解釋為「路；方向」，例如在電影中《空中救援》有句台詞：「Let me get outta your way.」（我先讓你過。）

　　Way 還有另一個常用的意思是「方式；方法」，例如你問別人：「Is there a way I can reach you?」（我要怎麼聯繫你？）還有主管要求你find some way（找到一些方法）解決問題。

和way相關片語及單字有way-out（解決之道）、all the way（整個途中；全部時間）、by the way（BTW；順便提起）、anyway（無論如何），相關用法請參閱以下例句。

1 Way n. 方式；方法
That's a nice way of putting it.
這說法真不錯。

2 All the way ph. 整個途中；全部時間
He was complaining all the way.
他一路上都在抱怨。

3 Way out ph. 解決之道
That's the easiest way out.
那是最簡單的解決之道。

4 By the way ph. 順道提起
By the way, how is your wife? Is she all right?
順便問一下，你太太怎麼樣？她還好嗎？

5 Anyway adv. 無論如何
That's about the extent of my Japanese anyway.
反正我的日文程度就這樣而已。

電影經典名言可以這樣應用

在工作場合中，當你發些小問題時說這句話，就表示真正的問題是更大的。

• **Just the tip of the iceberg.**
都只是冰山一角。　　　　　　　　　　　　　　　引自《實習大叔》

Unit 8　廠商來訪的應對進退

　　除了內部會議，你可能經常也需與外部廠商開會，例如供應商、外包廠商、自由工作者等，若遇到外國廠商，該如何溝通呢？

情境模擬對話篇

A A Mr. Ma is here to see you.
有位馬先生來找你。

B Take him to the meeting room.
帶他到會議室。

A Right this way.
這邊請。

A Have a seat. My boss will be with you in a moment.
請坐。我老闆馬上就來。

C Thank you.
謝謝！

A Would you like a drink? Coffee or tea?
你想喝點什麼？咖啡或茶？

C I'll take a water, though.
我喝水就好了。

A Ok, just a minute.
好的，請稍等。

B Thanks for stopping by.
多謝你過來。

C It's my pleasure.
這是我的榮幸。

B What would you like to show us today?
你今天想給我們展示什麼？

C I have a new product. Hang on real quick. Let me gear up my media.
我有一個新產品。等我一會兒！讓我安裝好設備。

B Do you need some help?
需要幫忙嗎？

C No...... All right. Why don't you give it a try?
不用，好了！要不你來試試？

C We shook hands on it.
我們握手說定了。

B Deal. Let me show you out.
成交！讓我送你出去。

從電影對話中找靈感

▶ They're here／They just got here.
他們到了／他們剛到。 ………………… 白宮風雲

▶ Could you just have a seat for a moment?
你能坐一下稍等片刻嗎？ ………………… 心靈捕手

▶ They're on their way now.
他們現在在路上。 ………………… 史帝夫賈伯斯

▶ I'll be down in a minute.
我馬上下來。 ………………… 因為愛你

▶ I'll meet you in the lobby in a few minutes.
幾分鐘後，我們大廳見。 ………………… 凸槌三人行

▶ I just came by to say hi.
我只是過來打個招呼。 .... 🎥 派特的幸福劇本

▶ It's so intrusive.
打擾了。 .... 🎥 與外婆同行

▶ Thanks for dropping down.
歡迎你到這兒來。 .... 🎥 實習大叔

▶ I'll be along in a minute.
我待會就過去。 .... 🎥 謎樣的雙眼

▶ I'm so thrilled to be here.
我很高興來這裡。 .... 🎥 實習大叔

▶ Just wait here a second.
在這等一下。 .... 🎥 凸槌三人行

▶ I'll be right out.
我馬上出去。 .... 🎥 非禮勿弒

最容易運用的職場關鍵字　Deal

　　Big deal 是「了不起的事情」，例如「It's really a big deal.」（真的很了不起。）反之，No big deal 或 Not a big deal 就是「沒什麼了不起」，例如：「It's no big deal.」（那沒什麼了不起。）這裡的 deal 解釋為「事情」。

　　在商用英文中，deal 最常用的意思是「交易」，例如：「This is a good deal.」（這是一個好的交易。）Deal 做動詞時意思是「交易；經營；對付」，例如：「Let's deal.」（談條件吧。）

　　和 deal 相關的片語，最常見的就是 deal with，意思是「對待；處理」，對人或對事都可以，例如他很難搞，就可以說：「He is hard to deal with.」，還有在電影《大賣空》中有句台詞：「Now you see what I had to deal with.」（現在你明白我有多費心了吧。）

　　由 deal 衍生出來的字有 dealer（業者；商人），例如 car dealer 就是「汽車經銷商」，在賭場發牌的荷官也叫 dealer，金融業在交易室

（dealing room）從事交易的人也叫dealer，相關用法請參閱以下例句。

1 **Deal** n. 交易
How many deals do we do a month?
我們一個月做多少筆交易？

2 **Deal with** ph. 處理
Haven't you dealt with that email yet?
你尚未處理那封電子郵件嗎？

3 **Dealer** n. 經銷商
This car dealer does not want to cut prices to sell.
這個汽車經銷商不願意降價出售。

百用句型

• It's very _____?
_____ 就是這樣。
① American（美國人）；
② Chinese（中國人）；
③ German（德國人）

電影經典名言可以這樣應用

在職場上，進行任何工作或計畫，若前期進行地還算順利時，就可以這麼說。

• **Well begun is half done.**
好的開始是成功的一半。

引自《大夢想家》

Unit 9　應對媒體的對話應用

　　企業偶爾會接受媒體訪問，有時是主動發送新聞，有時是面對媒體做危機處理，該如何用英文跟媒體溝通呢？讓我們看看下面例子。

情境模擬對話篇

A I work for China Times.
我是中國時報的記者。

B Just have a seat. What do you want to know?
請坐，你想知道什麼？

A Got a few questions. How did that happen yesterday?
我有幾個問題。昨天的事是怎麼發生的？

B It was an accident. It's all under control.
那是意外，一切都在控制之中。

A You want to elaborate on that?
你能詳細說明一下嗎？

B You are not recording this?
你沒錄音吧？

A I wouldn't do that without asking.
沒有你的允許我不會這麼做。

B The good news is we caught it in time.
好消息是我們即時發現了。

A Would you mind if I took some notes?
你介意我做一下紀錄嗎？

B I don't want you recording this in any way.
我不想你對這次談話做任何紀錄。

A Okay, this is off the record.
好的，這都不記錄。

B It's much bigger problem than that.
實際情況嚴重得多。

A How much bigger?
有多嚴重呢？

訪後結語

A Are we done?
問完了嗎？

B Thank you for the scoop.
謝謝你的獨家新聞。

從電影對話中找靈感

▶ But that wasn't the information I'm sharing with anybody.
不過這個祕密我沒跟任何人說。 ⋯⋯⋯⋯⋯⋯⋯⋯ 🎥 驚爆焦點

▶ Share it around if you like it.
如果你喜歡就分享給大家。 ⋯⋯⋯⋯⋯⋯⋯⋯⋯ 🎥 搖搖欲墜

▶ Can you tell me specifically what happened?
你可以具體地告訴我發生什麼了嗎？ ⋯⋯⋯⋯⋯ 🎥 驚爆焦點

▶ Put that away.
別記了。 ⋯⋯⋯⋯⋯⋯⋯⋯⋯⋯⋯⋯⋯⋯⋯⋯⋯⋯⋯ 🎥 驚爆焦點

▶ If it's not going to break the rules.
如果不觸犯規則的話。 ⋯⋯⋯⋯⋯⋯⋯⋯⋯⋯⋯⋯ 🎥 搖搖欲墜

▶ We can't sanitize this.
我們不能一筆帶過。 ⋯⋯⋯⋯⋯⋯⋯⋯⋯⋯⋯⋯⋯ 🎥 驚爆焦點

▶ I'm just follow up on one thing.
　我只是想再問清楚一件事。 ⋯⋯⋯⋯⋯⋯⋯⋯⋯⋯⋯⋯⋯⋯ 🎥 驚爆焦點

▶ I was wondering if I could ask you a few questions.
　我能不能問你幾個問題。 ⋯⋯⋯⋯⋯⋯⋯⋯⋯⋯⋯⋯⋯⋯ 🎥 驚爆焦點

▶ Do you really think it matters?
　你真的覺得這重要嗎？ ⋯⋯⋯⋯⋯⋯⋯⋯⋯⋯⋯⋯⋯⋯ 🎥 心靈大道

▶ You can sit in in the interview.
　你可以陪同採訪。 ⋯⋯⋯⋯⋯⋯⋯⋯⋯⋯⋯⋯⋯⋯⋯⋯ 🎥 驚爆焦點

▶ Why didn't he go public?
　為什麼他不公諸於眾？ ⋯⋯⋯⋯⋯⋯⋯⋯⋯⋯⋯⋯⋯⋯ 🎥 驚爆焦點

▶ You go ahead with your notes.
　你可以做紀錄。 ⋯⋯⋯⋯⋯⋯⋯⋯⋯⋯⋯⋯⋯⋯⋯⋯⋯ 🎥 驚爆焦點

▶ Where would I find it?
　我在哪裡可以找到？ ⋯⋯⋯⋯⋯⋯⋯⋯⋯⋯⋯⋯⋯⋯⋯ 🎥 驚爆焦點

最容易運用的職場關鍵字　Matter

　　當你感覺對方神情、臉色不對，想知道發生什麼問題，如果你是問：「Do you have any problems?」對方可能會回答：「I don't have any problem.」正確的問法應該是：「What's the matter with you?」（你怎麼了？）

　　Matter 做為名詞的意思是「事情；問題」，但做為動詞則解釋成「有關係；要緊」，例如「It doesn't matter.」（這不要緊）及「Does it matter?」（這重要嗎？）在電影《45年》中有句台詞：「What does it matter to you if I go or not?」（我去不去關你什麼事？）

　　英文有句饒舌的諺語：「Age is a matter of mind. If you don't mind, it doesn't matter.」前一句的 matter 和 mind 是名詞，意思是年齡是一件和心態有關的事情，後一句的 mind 和 matter 做動詞解，意思是如果你不介意，那就不要緊。其他和 matter 相關的用法請參閱以下例句。

1 Matter `n.` 麻煩事；毛病；問題
There's something the matter with this copy machine.
這台影印機有點問題。

2 Matter `n.` 事情；問題
It's not a matter of trying. It's what you have to do.
盡力是不夠的，這是你必須做到的。

3 Matter `v.` 有關係；要緊
All these things do not matter now.
所有這一切現在都無關緊要了。

4 No matter `ph.` 不論
The price remains the same, no matter where it is.
不論在什麼地方，價格都一樣。

5 As a matter of `ph.` 做為一個……事項
Please address their queries as a matter of urgency.
請提出他們的詢問並視之為緊急事項。

電影經典名言可以這樣應用

　　在職場中，這句話可以用在組織改變或轉換工作，鼓勵或說服別人時。

- **The thing in life that frightens us the most. Change.**
  人生中最嚇人的事。是改變。　　　　　　　　引自《實習大叔》

Unit 10　跟合作廠商討論報價費用

　　A公司的產品大賣，製造模具的廠商趁機調漲價格，於是兩家公司開始談判，讓我們看看如何用英文談？

情境模擬對話篇

A The price for our products goes up. It's very unfair to me.
我們產品的訂價上漲了，這對我很不公平。

B That's because costs are higher.
那是因為成本變高了。

A It seems like you're shaking us down.
你們似乎在敲詐我們。

B No, actually we've already lost a lot of money.
不，事實上我們已經虧了很多錢。

A How could that possibly be?
那怎麼可能呢？

B We have remade the molds then every other week.
我們每隔一周都要重新做一次模具。

A I think that's your mistakes. It's taking you four times to get right.
我想那是你們的錯誤，你做了四次才做對。

B It's very hard for us to lower the cost at this point.
我們現在很難降低成本。

A That's not the way you do business.
你們不應該這樣做生意的。

B It's only fair that you share the remaking cost, too.
你也要分擔重做的成本才算公平。

A Up to a third. You can afford to make less.
最多三分之一，你們少賺一點也能負擔啊！

B We can do 50% at most.
最多我們能負擔一半。

A Alright, I can agree under one condition.
好的，我能同意在一個條件之下。

B What is it?
什麼條件？

A The rate can't be changed within two years.
兩年內不能再調整價格。

B We'll shake on it.
我們握手成交。

從電影對話中找靈感

▶ I won't mince words with you.
我不和你兜圈子。 ………………………………………… 📹 因為愛你

▶ My offer still stands.
我的提議還是有效。 ………………………………………… 📹 驚爆焦點

▶ He makes pricing decisions.
他決定價格。 ……………………………………………… 📹 翻轉幸福

▶ To be honest, that's even gonna be hard to get.
說實話，那很難爭取到的。 ……………………………… 📹 翻轉幸福

▶ I just can't bring it to my boss.
我不能向老闆這樣提議。 ………………………………… 📹 翻轉幸福

▶ It's better than anything else out there.
它比市面上的都還要好。 ………………………………… 📹 翻轉幸福

▶ We are ready to meet your high expectations.
我們會讓你們滿意的。 ································· 凸槌三人行

▶ Numbers are just part of we have to take into account.
報價只是我們考慮的部分原因。 ······················ 凸槌三人行

▶ Hopefully, this is the closed deal.
希望我們已經成交。 ································· 凸槌三人行

▶ We have to sweeten the package.
我們必須提出更吸引人的條件。 ······················ 凸槌三人行

▶ I understand and appreciate your position.
我們理解也尊重你的立場。 ··························· 人質

▶ It was my understanding that we were done.
我本以為我們已經說好了。 ·························· 凸槌三人行

▶ You got a strong number set.
你們的報價很有競爭力。 ···························· 凸槌三人行

▶ That's just the bottom line.
那是底線。 ·· 凸槌三人行

▶ Was a pleasure doing business with you.
很高興和你做生意。 ······························· 時空永恆的愛戀

▶ Why don't we cut the shit?
我們有話就直說吧！ ······························· 家有兩個爸

▶ If you can please sign this, we'll be done over there.
請你簽一下字，我們那邊就完成了。 ··················· 心靈大道

▶ That's the deal.
那就這麼說定了。 ·································· 心靈大道

▶ It's nice to be in business with you.
很高興能與你合作。 ······························· 搖搖欲墜

▶ That's the rate. Fair enough.
就這個價錢，還行吧！ ····························· 命運鞋奏曲

▶ Don't "lawyer" me.
別跟我來律師那一套。 ………………………………………… 🎥 出棋制勝

▶ Sharpen your pencils. I'll get the paperwork ready.
準備好簽名吧！我來準備好文件。 ………………………… 🎥 大賣空

▶ Can we see some of your offering documents?
我們能看看你們的交易說明書嗎？ ………………………… 🎥 大賣空

▶ He's cornered the market.
他壟斷了市場。 …………………………………………………… 🎥 聖母峰

▶ Are you gonna keep me in suspense?
你在吊我胃口嗎？ …………………………………………………… 🎥 機械姬

▶ He's after something better.
他另有盤算。 🎥 白宮風雲

▶ It's standard. Take your time. Read it over.
這是標準格式，不急，仔細閱讀。 ……………………… 🎥 機械姬

▶ That's daylight robbery.
光天化日下搶錢啊！ …………………………………………… 🎥 聖母峰

最容易運用的職場關鍵字 | Share

　　Share 做為動詞的意思是「分享；分擔；共同享有」，例如share your ideas（分享你的想法）、share a room（合住一間房間）、share the duties（分擔責任）。Share 做為名詞的意思是「一份；股份；市場佔有率」。

　　由share所衍生出來的名詞有market share 及 shared folder。Market share的意思是「市場佔有率」，係指某一時間，某家公司的業務規模或某項產品，在相同產業或同類產品銷售額中所佔的比例。

　　Shared folder的意思是「共享的檔案夾」，在公司的內部網路裡，通常可以建立shared folder，但只有部門內同仁可以使用，大家把相關檔案放在shared folder，互相分享資料，增加工作效率並保存檔案。

　　Share 做為股份或股票時，可以衍生出shareholder（股東），例如在

電影《我想念我自己》中有句台詞：「We're sort of shareholders.」（我們有點像股東。）相關用法請參閱以下例句。

1 Share v. 分享
I am under no obligation to share that information.
我沒有義務分享你那個訊息。

2 Share n. 股份；股票
Our company's shares can be traded in the secondary market right now.
我們公司的股票現在可以在次級市場上交易了。

3 Market share ph. 市場佔有率；市場份額
We should be tracking our market share very closely.
我們應該非常密切地追蹤我們的市場佔有率。

4 Shared folder n. 共享檔案夾
You can find the softcopy in the shared folder.
你可以在共享檔案夾中找到檔案。

電影經典名言可以這樣應用

　　這句話可以用在建議別人在出差或社交中可以多認識些人以增廣見聞及增加人脈。

• **Sometimes it's nice to talk to people who don't know your auntie.**
有時候能和陌生人聊聊也蠻好的。　　　　　　　　引自《布魯克林》

解答／十句常用開會談判的英譯

1. He does make a valid point.

2. It's not a high priority.

3. How do you propose we do that?

4. What's in it for me?

5. You're blowing this all out of the proportion.

6. Why are you so bossy?

7. Don't take it personally.

8. It's an once-in-a-lifetime deal.

9. We shook hands on it.

10. It seems like you're shaking us down.

第 **4** 章

出國洽公的
常用對話

試試看下列幾句出差常用的句子,如何用英文表達?

1. 你要出差嗎?
2. 我們什麼時候出發?
3. 從這兒到芝加哥的實際飛航時間是多久?
4. 從你的口音能聽出來。
5. 你有沒有零錢可以找100元?
6. 我用楊凱文的名字預約。
7. 我能要一張這城市的免費地圖嗎?
8. 天啊!我們多久沒聯絡了?
9. 有洗手間能借用一下嗎?
10.這附近有什麼值得去的景點嗎?

(答案在本章最後一頁)

Unit 1　行前準備的閒聊

　　B先生準備早點下班，因為明天要出差去東京，他同事A先生不知道他要出差，下班前和他聊了一下，詢問他出差的細節。

情境模擬對話篇

B I'll get off of work early today. I have to pack.
我今天要早點下班。我得收拾行李。

A Are you going on a business trip?
你要出差嗎？

B Yep. I'm heading out tomorrow morning. I'm flying up to Tokyo for a meeting.
是的，我明早就得出發。我要飛到東京開會。

A Wow! How long will it take by plane?
哇，要飛多久啊？

B It's just a three-hour flight.
坐飛機只要三小時。

A Would you like to hear our itinerary?
想聽聽我們的行程嗎？

B Sure. Go ahead!
當然，快說！

繼續閒聊

A I'll give me an opportunity to catch a baseball game.
我會順便去看場棒球比賽。

B You're gonna have a lovely time. Don't forget to send your pix on Instagram.
你一定會很開心的，別忘了在Instagram上發你的照片。

A Will do.
我會的。

B Why don't I take you up to airport?
何不讓我送你去機場？

A No need. My family will send me there. Thanks anyway.
不需要，我家人會送我去，無論如何謝謝你。

B Please be safe over there. Call me when you get there.
到那裡要注意安全，到了打電話給我。

A I will. I am off.
我會的。我走了。

B Have a safe flight.
一路順風！

從電影對話中找靈感

▶ What time we heading out?
我們什麼時候出發？ ·· 🎥 加州大地震

▶ We can head up to Seattle right after.
之後我們可以去西雅圖。 ··································· 🎥 加州大地震

▶ What's the ETA（estimated time of arrival）?
預估到達的時間是？ ······································· 🎥 紙上城市

▶ I'd like to make a reservation for the next available flight from Cobh to New York.
我要預訂最近一班從科芙飛紐約的機票。 ············ 🎥 布魯克林

▶ How long have we been driving?
我們開多久了？ ··· 🎥 紙上城市

▶ They're setting it up when we get there.
他們會做好準備迎接我們。............................ 📹 聖母峰

▶ I will call you when we land.
飛機降落時，我會打電話給你。.................... 📹 空中救援

▶ Are you on the early train?
你要搭早班的火車嗎？................................ 📹 布魯克林

▶ I'm booked to go back to New York on twenty-first.
我回紐約的機票是21號。............................. 📹 布魯克林

▶ I'm away to America.
我要動身去美國了。..................................... 📹 布魯克林

▶ You can wait an extra week.
你可以多待一周。.. 📹 布魯克林

最容易運用的職場關鍵字 Get

當老闆交代你事情後，可以簡單回覆：「Got it.」（知道了。）當你對部屬或同事說明一件事數次，對方還是沒聽懂，就會有點生氣地說：「You still don't get it?」（你還是不懂嗎？）Get這個字是動詞，主要的意思有「收到；獲得；到達；搭乘；明白」。

Get可說是萬用動詞，例如get hurt是「受傷」，get後面也可以加介系詞，例如生氣的時候會說：「Get out of my office.」（滾出我的辦公室。）或「Get out of my sight.」（滾出我的視線之外。）不要以為這麼不客氣的話不會出現在辦公室，我曾看過一位台灣主管，把他的外國主管趕出他的辦公室時，就說了這句話，事後才知道他是在演戲，他說對付老外，有時候必須這樣。其他和get相關的片語及用法請參閱以下例句。

英文	中譯	英文	中譯
Get off	動身；下車	Get by	維持
Get rid of	消除	Get used to	習慣

1 **Get on with** ph. 繼續做某事
Can we get on with the meeting now?
我們現在可以繼續開會了嗎？

2 **Get into trouble** ph. 陷入困境；惹上麻煩
Are you intending to get us into trouble?
你想讓我們陷入困境嗎？

3 **Get through** ph. 辦完；完成
When you get through with your work, let's go out for a drink.
當你完成工作後，我們出去喝一杯吧！

4 **Get back to sb.** ph. 回覆
I'll get back to you later.
我晚點再回覆你。

5 **Get over** ph. 克服；熬過
He was disappointed at not getting the job, but he'll get over it.
他因沒得到那份工作而感到失望，不過他能熬過去的。

電影經典名言可以這樣應用

　　這句話可以用來鼓勵別人，尤其是當他們追求夢想時遭遇阻礙時。

- **You can't let the practical get you down. You gotta keep going to what you love.**
你不能被現實擊倒，你要不斷追逐你喜愛的事。　引自《翻轉幸福》

Unit 2　機場櫃檯辦理登機的相關對話

到航空公司辦理登機，櫃檯小姐會詢問託運行李、座位偏好及提醒登機時間、位置。

情境模擬對話篇

A Good evening, sir. Welcome to Canada Airline.
晚安先生，歡迎來到加拿大航空。

B I'm checking in.
我要辦理登機。

A Where（are）you headed?
你要去哪裡？

B I'm headed to Singapore. Here is my passport.
我要飛往新加坡，這是我的護照。

A How many pieces of luggage do you want to check in?
你有幾件行李要登記託運？

B Just one.
就這件。

A Please put them on the scales. Is there any lithium batteries or lighters in your luggage?
請把它們放在磅秤上，行李裡面有任何的鋰電池或打火機嗎？

B No.
沒有。

A Would you like a window or an aisle seat, sir?
先生，您想要靠窗或靠走道的位子？

B Aisle seat, please. Is the plane on schedule?
麻煩靠走道。飛機會準時起飛嗎？

A Yes, your flight is on time.
是的，班機會準時起飛！

B Great!
太好了！

A Okay, you're all set. Here is your boarding pass. You have seat 21C. Your flight leaves at gate 5, and boarding starts at 9:30. Enjoy your fight!
好的，手續都好了，這是你的登機證。你的座位號碼是21C，請由5號閘口登機，九點三十分開始登機。祝飛行愉快！

B Thank you.
謝謝。

從電影對話中找靈感

▶ That all you got?
你的行李就這些？ ··· 🎥 聖母峰

▶ And we'll be all set.
沒其他手續了。 ·· 🎥 安諾瑪麗莎

▶ Here you go, sir.
好了，先生。 ·· 🎥 空中救援

▶ We've a seat by the window all picked out for you.
我們特別為你挑選靠窗座位。 ··································· 🎥 空中救援

▶ Do you have any preferences, sir?
先生，您（對座位）有什麼偏好嗎？ ·························· 🎥 白宮風雲

▶ May I see your ticket and photo ID?
可以看一下您的機票及有照片的身分證明嗎？ ·············· 🎥 白宮風雲

▶ What's the actual flying time from here to Chicago?
從這兒到芝加哥的實際飛航時間是多久？ ···················· 🎥 白宮風雲

最容易運用的職場關鍵字　Head

之前在服務的公司裡，有位奉派來台成立保險公司的英國佬，初期目標就是要找齊保險業務成員。有次他在報告時說：「I have good news. Our headcount increased 100% last week.」（我有好消息，我們的員工總數增加了100%。）停了一下子又說：「From one to two.」（從一位變成兩位。）雖然他才招募一人，但以成長率來說是100%，多麼正面且幽默的講法，果然博得哄堂大笑。

Head在職場上是指一個部門或公司的最高主管，例如Head of Legal & Compliance（法令遵循部門主管）、Finance head（財務部門主管）。一個部門的headcount，就是這個部門的員工總數，當外在環境不佳時，公司通常會實行「headcount freeze」（人事凍結）。

和head相關的片語，在職場上常用的還有heads up，意思是「提醒；注意；警覺」，例如對於別人提醒你，你可以回覆：「Thanks for the heads-up.」（謝謝你的提醒。）其他和head相關的用法請參閱以下例句。

1 Head n. 頭；腦
What's the first word that pops into your head?
在你腦子裡浮現的第一個字是什麼？

2 Headline n. 頭條新聞；標題
Today's newspaper headline caught his attention.
今天報紙的頭條新聞引起他的注意。

3 Headcount n. 總人數
Most companies are headcount freeze due to the financial crisis.
由於金融危機的影響，大多數公司都凍結人事。

4 Headhunter n. 獵人頭公司
You can try to find a job through headhunters.
你可以嘗試透過獵人頭公司找工作。

5 **Heads up** ph. 提醒；注意；警覺
You keep your head up.
你自己小心。

電影經典名言可以這樣應用

在職場上，主管對部屬訓誡時，這些話也可以派上用場。

• Not standing where you thought you would, hoped to and
asking the questions, "What could I have done differently?
Could I have led better?" The only thing you can do when
things go against you is pick yourself up and push back.
不要站在那裡認為你會或你希望，期望要問自己：「我能有什麼不同
表現？我能做得更好嗎？」當事情不如意時，唯一你能做的是：振
作精神及擊退逆境。　　　　　　　　　　　　　　　引自《凸槌三人行》

Unit 3　國外入境的對話應用

　　在海關辦理入境時，若你是到已開發的國家，不純粹是短程旅遊，海關通常會很仔細地盤問，因為他們會擔心你可能會非法居留或非法工作，所以一定會釐清本單元涉及的問題後才會放行。

情境模擬對話篇

B Could you please step forward?
麻煩你上前一步？

B May I see your passport and immigration form, please?
麻煩讓我看一下你的護照和入境表格。

A Of course. Here you are.
沒問題，給你。

B What brought you here?
你來這裡做什麼？

A I am here on business.
我是來出差的。

B What do you do?
你從事什麼行業的？

A I freelance a little for consulting firms.
我是自由工作者，為諮詢顧問公司提供一些服務。

B How long do you plan to stay?
你計畫停留多久？

A About three weeks.
三個禮拜左右。

B Where will you be staying?
你會住在哪裡？

A I will be staying at Hilton hotel.
我會住在希爾頓飯店。

B How much cash are you carrying?
你帶多少現金？

A Around two thousand US dollar.
大約兩千美元。

B Here is your passport.
護照還你。

A Thanks a lot.
非常感謝。

海關常問問題

1 Do you come alone? Any companions?
你一個人來嗎？有同伴嗎？

2 What is the purpose of your visit?
你來這裡的目的是什麼？

3 When was the picture on the passport taken?
護照上的照片是什麼時候拍的？

4 Have you confirmed your return ticket?
你的回程機票訂好了嗎？

5 What is your occupation/ What line of business are you in?
你從事什麼行業？

6 Do you have anything to declare?
你有任何東西要申報嗎？

最容易運用的職場關鍵字　**Bring**

有次一位國外的同事突然出現在我們的辦公室，我心裡第一句想問：「什麼風把你吹來？」但卻不知道英文該怎麼說？只說：「Hi, Brandon.」後來才知道應該說：「What brings you here?」當時我的另一位英文很好的同事，立即說：「What are you doing here?」（你怎麼會在這裡？）外國同事笑笑回答：「Good question.」（好問題。）

Bring最簡單的意思是「帶來」，可以帶人或物，在職場上還常聽到其他用法，例如bring back the number（把數字帶回來），意思就是讓業績好起來。Bring的衍生之意還有「引起；導致；促使」，例如：「What brought you to say that?」（你為何說那樣的話？）其他和bring相關的用法請參閱以下例句。

---

1 Bring v. 帶著

I am going to go on my sun-sea and relax holiday tomorrow and will NOT bring my laptop.

我明天將要展開我的海灘陽光放鬆假期，而且不會帶著我的筆記型電腦。

---

2 Bring in ph. 獲利

His coffee shop brings in half a million a year.

他的咖啡店每年獲利五十萬元。

---

3 Bring up ph. 提起；提出

These are matters that you can bring up in committee.

這些問題你可在委員會中提出。

---

4 Bring down ph. 減少

We have to bring down the room and people will be on work bench kind.

我們必須減少空間，大家將在類似工作平台的地方工作。

5 **Bring into effect** ph. 實行；使生效
A new system of taxation will be brought into effect next year.
新的稅收制度將於明年實行。

百用句型

• Is there ＿＿＿＿＿＿＿＿ near here／around here／nearby?
這附近有 ＿＿＿＿＿＿＿＿ 嗎？

①a pay phone（投幣電話）；
②a currency exchange location（換匯的地方）；
③any stores selling prepaid cell phone cards（任何商家銷售手機預付卡）；
④a 7-Eleven store（7-11便利商店）

電影經典名言可以這樣應用

　　這句話可以用在鼓勵別人，有些事情雖然最終結果不如預期，但從過程中仍然可以學到寶貴的經驗。

• **I believe the journey to be more important than the destination.**
我相信過程比目的地更重要。　　　　　　　　引自《全面進化》

Unit 4　在國外搭計程車的對話應用

出差時交通費多半都能報公帳，到了人生地不熟的地方，搭計程車會是最方便的。

情境模擬對話篇

A Where（are）you off to?
你要去哪裡？

B Please take me to the IFC（International Finance Centre）.
Here's the address. How long will it take to reach there?
請載我到國際金融中心，這是地址，到那裡需要多久？

A It's about 40 minutes. Is this your first time in Hong Kong?
大約40分鐘，您第一次來香港嗎？

B Once before. Four years ago.
以前來過一次，四年前來的。

A It's changed since then. You ought to check it out.
這些年變化很大，你應該四處轉轉。

B I'll try to.
我會的。

A Where are you from? Taiwan?
你從哪裡來的？台灣嗎？

B How do you know that?
你怎麼知道？

A I can tell by your accent.
從你的口音能聽出來。

B You are amazing.
你好厲害喔！

A There's a lot to see in the city. You can watch Hong Kong night view from Victoria Peak.
這城市有很多景點，你可以從太平山上看香港夜景。

B That sounds fascinating.
聽起來好極了！

A There it is. The fare comes to $150.
到了，車資是港幣150元。

B May I have a receipt?
我可以要一張收據嗎？

A Sure. Here you go.
好的，給你收據。

跟計程車司機交談的參考語句

1 Where to?（Where would you like to go? Where do you want to go?）
您要到哪兒去？

2 Do you have change for $100?
你有沒有零錢可以找一百元？

3 That's a lot of times.
很多次啊！

4 How long are you visiting Singapore?
你要在新加坡待多久？

5 Would you please turn up the air-conditioner?
請把冷氣開大一點好嗎？

6 Would you please turn down your radio? I'd make a phone call.

請你把收音機音量關小一點好嗎？我要打電話。

7 What's that big beautiful building over there?
那棟漂亮的建築物是什麼？

8 What can I buy to take home from Singapore?
在新加坡我可以買什麼帶回家？

9 It was nice talking to you.
跟你談話真有趣。

10 Just leave me on the corner of market.
讓我在市場轉彎處下車。

11 How much is the fare?
車資多少？

百用句型

• Where's a good place to buy _____ ?
哪裡是購買 _____ 的好地方？

①shoes（鞋子）；
②local products（土產）；
③3C products（3C產品）

最容易運用的職場關鍵字 | **Try**

　　在職場上，我們經常會鼓勵同事說：「你就try看看嘛！不try怎麼知道不行。」Try這個字可以做為動詞及名詞，意思都是「嘗試；試圖；努力」，例如問：「Who'd like to have a try at it?」（誰想試試呢？）

　　Try one's best的意思是「盡某人最大的努力」，和do one's best意思相同，例如：「Danny will try his best to finish the new book.」（丹尼會

盡最大努力完成這本新書。）Try on的意思是「試穿；試用」，例如逛街時問店員：「Can I try it on?」（我可以試穿嗎？）

　　由try所衍生出來的字有trial，意思是「嘗試；努力；試用；試驗」，生技醫藥產業常會用到trial這個字，例如Clinical Trial（臨床試驗）。和trial相關的片語有trial and error，意思是「試誤法」，就是在嘗試的過程中，選擇一個可能的解法，如果失敗就再選擇另一個的解法，直到找到最適合的解法。其他和try相關的用法請參閱以下例句。

1 Try v. 嘗試；試圖；努力
This idea seems good but you need to try it out
這個想法似乎不錯，但你需要試驗一下。

2 Try one's best ph. 盡某人的全力
The team will always try their best in assisting these requests to be turnaround ASAP.
我們團隊總會盡全力協助這些要求，讓情況盡快好轉。

3 Trial and error ph. 嘗試錯誤；反覆試驗
He learned technical skills by trial and error.
他透過不斷地摸索掌握技能。

4 Try on ph. 耍弄
It's no use trying on such tricks with us.
跟我們耍這種花招是沒用的。

<table>
<tr><td>Unit
5</td><td>國外住房登記的對話應用</td></tr>
</table>

　　到國外出差，出海關外第一件事通常就是先到住宿飯店check-in，
那辦理住房登記時會用到哪些英文呢？

情境模擬對話篇

A Good afternoon, sir. Can I help you?
先生您好，我能為您效勞嗎？

B I'd like to check in.
我要入住。

A Do you have a reservation?
您有預訂房間嗎？

B Yes, I have a reservation under Kevin Yang.
有，我用楊凱文的名字預約。

A Just a moment, please. And you'll be with us for just one night, sir?
請等一下！先生您就住一晚嗎？

B Yes, I'm just here for a day.
是的，我只在這裡停留一天。

A May I have your ID and credit card? I'm just need to make an imprint of your credit card, for incidentals.
可以給我您的身分證件及信用卡嗎？
我需要複印一下信用卡，用於雜費。

B Here you are.
給你。

A Will you fill out this form and sign here, please?
請您填好這份表格並在這裡簽名。

A Perfect. So it's all set then. Here are the room keys and breakfast vouchers.
太好了，所以手續都辦好了。這是房間鑰匙和早餐券。

B What's the check-out time?
退房時間是幾點？

A Checkout's 11:00 a.m.
早上十一點以前退房。

B Can I get a free map of this city?
我能要張這城市的免費地圖嗎？

A Sorry, we just ran out of free maps.
抱歉，我們的免費地圖剛剛用完了。

從電影對話中找靈感

▶ It's good to be here at the Mandarin Oriental.
很高興來到文華東方酒店。 ·········· 🎥 丹尼柯林斯

▶ Can you please initial here? To say you acknowledge that.
請您在這兒簡略簽名（簽姓名字母的首字）？以表明你已知道這些規定。 ·········· 🎥 凸槌三人行

▶ I'm afraid your credit card is not working.
你的信用卡恐怕無法使用了。 ·········· 🎥 凸槌三人行

▶ Your credit card has been denied.
你的信用卡被拒絕了。 ·········· 🎥 天菜大廚

▶ Can I see your dollar exchange ratio?
我可以看一下你的美元兌換匯率嗎？ ·········· 🎥 凸槌三人行

▶ Let me check with the front desk.
我向前台查詢一下。 ·········· 🎥 心靈大道

137

▶ Could you please order me a cab?
你可以幫我叫輛計程車嗎？ ··· 🎥◀ 大夢想家

▶ We need to find an electronics store.
我們需要找一家電器店。 ·· 🎥◀ 加州大地震

最容易運用的職場關鍵字 | Check

　　Check常用於到國外出差入住及離開飯店時，例如check in（到達並登記；報到）及check out（結帳離開；檢查），還有當你用完餐要結帳時可以說：「Check, please?」或「May I have the check, please?」

　　由check所衍生在職場常用的字或片語也不少，例如Checklist的意思是「檢查表；核對清單」，例如在產品出廠之前，品管人員會拿著checklist逐一核對是否都能通過檢驗。又如Sampling check的意思是「抽樣檢查」，例如製造一百件產品，隨機抽樣十件，若都沒問題，代表其他出錯的概率就很小了。還有Spot check的意思是「進行抽查」，就是不預警地突襲檢查，以確認員工隨時都能保持高的工作水準，其他和check相關的用法請參閱以下例句。

1 Check v. 檢查
I'll check it out.
我會查查看。

2 Check v. 確認；核對
Please help check if the schedule fits yours.
請幫忙確認這時間是否適合你。

3 Check n. 支票
Can I pay by check?
我可以付支票嗎？

4 Checklist n. 清單；檢查表
Please review the attached summary report and investigation checklist.
請仔細閱讀所附的總結報告和調查清單。

5 Double-check ph. 覆核；再次檢查／確認
I would like to double-check if you have forwarded the notice to your customers before.
我想再次確認你之前是否已經轉發通知給你的客戶。

6 Check up on ph. 調查某人或某事
I'm calling to check up on you.
我打來是要問你好不好。

電影經典名言可以這樣應用

　　在職場上，這句話可以用來告誡部屬做事要謹慎細心，不要忽略任何小細節。

- **It's the little things that'll trip you.**
　細節決定成敗。　　　　　　　　　　　　　　　引自《時空永恆的愛戀》

Unit 6 異地相逢的老友敘舊

　　出差工作之餘,總會想找認識的朋友或同事敘敘舊,也可打發一些時間。

情境模擬對話篇

A Hello!
哈囉!

B Jerry, it's you?
傑瑞,是你嗎?

A Who is this?
你是誰?

B I'm Kevin, from Taiwan.
我是凱文,從台灣來的。

A Hi Kevin. I didn't recognize your voice.
嗨,凱文,我沒認出你的聲音。

B I'm in New York on business.
我到紐約出差。

A Jesus, how long has it been?
天啊!我們多久沒聯絡了?

B Three or four years. Do you want to get a drink? Let's catch up.
三、四年了吧!你想一起喝一杯嗎?讓我們敘敘舊!

A I'd love to. But I can't stay very long, I have to go to work early tomorrow.
我很樂意,但我不能待太久,我明天得很早去上班。

B No problem. It'll be lovely to see you.
沒問題。見到你肯定會很高興。

A Talk to you later.
待會聊！

A Kevin. It's really lovely to see you.
凱文，見到你太高興了！

B It's been so long. How have you been?
真的是好久沒聯繫了，你最近過得怎麼樣？

A Same old. You?
老樣子。你呢？

B I'm pretty good.
我很好。

從電影對話中找靈感

▶ Tell me what's going on.
告訴我近況。 ⋯⋯⋯⋯⋯⋯⋯⋯⋯⋯⋯⋯⋯⋯ 🎥 安諾瑪麗莎

▶ Not too much.
沒什麼。 ⋯⋯⋯⋯⋯⋯⋯⋯⋯⋯⋯⋯⋯⋯⋯⋯⋯ 🎥 家有兩個爸

▶ I've gained some weight.
我變胖了。 ⋯⋯⋯⋯⋯⋯⋯⋯⋯⋯⋯⋯⋯⋯⋯⋯ 🎥 安諾瑪麗莎

▶ It doesn't matter. It's all water under the bridge.
沒關係。都是過去的事了。 ⋯⋯⋯⋯⋯⋯⋯⋯⋯ 🎥 安諾瑪麗莎

▶ It's like out of the blue.
這事太突然了。 ⋯⋯⋯⋯⋯⋯⋯⋯⋯⋯⋯⋯⋯⋯ 🎥 安諾瑪麗莎

▶ At least you're making a good living.
至少你過得很不錯。 ⋯⋯⋯⋯⋯⋯⋯⋯⋯⋯⋯⋯ 🎥 無處可逃

▶ But things kind of shifted.
但事情後來發生了變化。……………………………… 🎥 安諾瑪麗莎

▶ It's hard to explain.
很難解釋。…………………………………………… 🎥 安諾瑪麗莎

換種說法也可通

中譯	常用說法	另類說法
祝你一路順風！	Have a safe trip!	Godspeed.《白宮風雲》
我沒有祕密。	I have no secret.	I am an open book.《飢餓遊戲》
我們必須趕時間了。	We're gonna have to leave.	We're gonna have to haul ass. 《凸槌三人行》
飛行不是我的專長。	I'm not good at flying.	Flying is not my cup of tea. 《空中救援》

百用句型（問路）

Excuse me. 對不起！

• Do you know where ＿＿＿＿＿＿＿＿ is?
　請問你知道 ＿＿＿＿＿＿ 在哪裡嗎？

• Can you tell me the way to ＿＿＿＿＿＿＿ ?
　可以告訴我怎麼去 ＿＿＿＿＿ 嗎？

• Do you know how to get to ＿＿＿＿＿＿＿ ?
　你知道怎麼去 ＿＿＿＿＿ 嗎？

最容易運用的職場關鍵字　Catch

　　有次在上one-on-one（一對一）英文課時，老師的手機突然響了，他接起電話告訴對方他正在上課，最後說了一句「Catch you later.」（稍後再聊），和Call you later意思相似，在這裡catch就是talk或contact的意思。

　　在商用英文中，catch則常解釋為「吸引；理解；聽清楚」，例如老闆批評你設計的廣告看板，無法catch customer's attention（無法吸引客戶的注意力）。

　　與catch相關的片語最常見就是catch up，第一種意思是「了解情況、趕上進度」，在電影《派特的幸福劇本》中有句台詞：「I'm sorry it took so long for me to catch up.」（很抱歉我花了這麼多時間才了解。）

　　另一種意思是「敘舊」，例如「Let's catch up next week.」（讓我們下週敘敘舊。）在多部電影中的台詞常出現：「I'm gonna catch up with you.」（我待會再過來找你）或「Can I catch up to you?」（我能來找你嗎？）其他和catch相關的用法請參閱以下例句。

1 Catch v. 理解；聽清楚
Roger didn't catch what the boss said.
羅傑沒有聽清楚老闆說的話。

2 Catch v. 吸引；抓住
Your presentation should try to catch the audience's attention.
你的簡報應該試圖抓住觀眾的注意力。

3 Catch up ph. 敘舊
I will fix some time to catch up with you when I am in Kuala Lumpur this month.
當我這個月在吉隆坡時，我會喬出時間和你敘敘舊。

4 Catch up with ph. 趕上

You have to work hard in order to catch up with the rest of the department.

你必須努力工作以趕上部門其他同事。

電影經典名言可以這樣應用

這句話的意思是工作態度是決定事情能否做好的關鍵。

- **It's not the altitude, it's the attitude.**
  態度決定一切，不是高度。

引自《聖母峰》

Unit 7　造訪客戶時的櫃檯應對

　　出差若不是到區域總部或總公司，便是去拜訪廠商或客戶，到廠商大樓 Lobby 的接待處該如何應對？

情境模擬對話篇

在大廳

B What can I do for you?
有何貴幹？

A I'm here to see Mr. Brown. My name is Kevin Yang.
我來這裡見伯朗先生。我叫楊凱文。

B Can I see some ID?
我可以看一下身份證明文件嗎？

A Here you are.
給你。

B Here is your temporary visitor card. Sign in, please.
這是你的臨時訪問卡，請簽名。

A Okay.
好的！

B Does he know who you are if I call his office?
如果我打給他的辦公室，他會知道你是誰嗎？

A Of course he know.
他當然知道。

B He's on the call. Please have a seat.
他在電話中，請先坐一下。

（電話接通）Mr. Brown, you got a guest down here.
伯朗先生，您樓下有訪客。

B Sorry to keep you waiting. Please take the elevator up to 13/F.
抱歉讓你久等了。請搭電梯到十三樓。

祕書接待處

A I'm here to see Mr. Brown.
我來這裡見伯朗先生。

C Mr. Yang. He's expecting you. You can go right in.
楊先生，他在等你了，你可以直接進去。

A Thank you.
謝謝！

從電影對話中找靈感

▶ He didn't show for work today.
他今天沒上班。⋯⋯⋯⋯⋯⋯⋯⋯⋯⋯ 心靈捕手

▶ Do you expect him back soon?
你預估他很快會回來嗎？⋯⋯⋯⋯⋯⋯ 命運鞋奏曲

▶ We have to push your meeting.
我們不得不延期你們的會議。⋯⋯⋯⋯ 凸槌三人行

▶ I'll visit when it's more appropriate.
我會等更合適的時間再來拜訪。⋯⋯⋯ 心靈大道

▶ He's not expecting me.
他不知道我會來。⋯⋯⋯⋯⋯⋯⋯⋯⋯ 時空永恆的愛戀

▶ Of course. Please take a seat over there.
好的，請在那邊坐一下。⋯⋯⋯⋯⋯⋯ 丹麥女孩

▶ As a foreign guest, you'll need to be accompanied.
外國賓客必須隨時有人陪同。 ⋯⋯⋯⋯⋯⋯⋯⋯⋯⋯⋯⋯⋯ 🎥◀ 詭影任務

▶ Mr. Chen will see you now.
陳先生可以見你了。 ⋯⋯⋯⋯⋯⋯⋯⋯⋯⋯⋯⋯⋯⋯⋯⋯⋯ 🎥◀ 加州大地震

▶ I don't know anyone around here by that name.
我不認識這裡有叫那個名字的人。 ⋯⋯⋯⋯⋯⋯⋯⋯⋯⋯ 🎥◀ 當辣妹來敲門

▶ I'm gonna tell her that it's not a good time.
我去跟她說現在不方便。 ⋯⋯⋯⋯⋯⋯⋯⋯⋯⋯⋯⋯⋯⋯⋯ 🎥◀ 加州大地震

百用句型

- I am here to _____ .
  我來這裡 _____ 。
  ①see Mr. Smith（見史密斯先生）；
  ②give a presentation（做簡報）；
  ③apply for the job（應徵工作）

最容易運用的職場關鍵字　**Keep**

　　當你要求部屬做進度報告或隨時讓你知道事情的發展，都可以說：「Keep me posted.」或「Keep me informed.」意思是「有任何消息記得通知我」或「有新的進度記得向我報告」。

　　此外，在email或對話結束時，常會說Keep in touch，也可以用Stay in touch，意思都是「保持聯絡」，這可以是客套話，也可以是真的希望對方再和你聯絡，端看對象是誰。

　　和keep相關的片語，常用的有keep in mind（記住），也可以用bear in mind。還有keep an eye on（仔細看好；細心照顧）及keep something to oneself（保密）。其他和keep相關的用法請參閱以下例句。

1 **Keep** v. 保留
Remember to keep email as proof.
記得保留電子郵件做為證明。

2 **Keep** v. 繼續；持續
We suggest to keep doing this business.
我們建議繼續做這項業務。

3 **Keep in mind** ph. 記住；放在心上
You have to arrive by eleven o'clock. Keep that in mind.
你得在十一點以前到達，記住這一點。

4 **Keep an eye on** ph. 仔細看守好；細心照顧；監視
Could you keep an eye on my luggage for a moment?
你能幫我看一會兒行李嗎？

5 **Keep something to yourself** ph. 保密
I want you to keep this news to yourself.
我要求你對這個消息保密。

電影經典名言可以這樣應用

在職場上，當有同事高談闊論、不切實際時，就可以說這句話回應。

- **That's easier said than done.**
  說比做容易。

引自《派特的幸福劇本》

Unit 8　初次與受訪者見面的常用對話

　　見到想要拜訪的人，雙方必然會先禮貌性問候，聊一下旅途狀況，記得可先試著誇讚一下對方的辦公室陳列等。

情境模擬對話篇

B Hi, Kevin. Why don't you come on in?
嗨，凱文，快請進！

A I like what you've done with the place. What is that?
我喜歡你這邊的裝潢，那是什麼？

B That's an antique.
那是古董。

A It's quite unusual and must worth a fortune.
這非常特別，一定很值錢！

B How was your flight?
飛行還順利吧？

A It was fine. A little bumpy. I only landed a couple hours ago.
還好，有點顛簸！我幾個小時前才下飛機。

B And the jet lag?
有時差嗎？

A I'm pretty jetlagged.
我有時差。

B That first night can be brutal.
第一晚通常很難熬。

A I'm in a little bit of a fog now. But I think I can survive.
我現在有點暈暈的，但我想我能熬過去的。

B You must be exhausted after your trip. You want something to eat or drink?
坐了這麼久的飛機，你一定累壞了吧！你要吃點或喝點什麼嗎？

A Black coffee, please.
請給我純咖啡。

B Let me show you around.
讓我帶你轉轉。

A Not a bad view.
風景還不錯。

B You have a bit of fun while you're here.
你在這裡的時候可以找點樂子。

A I've done my research.
我已經做好功課了。

B You are really something. Hope you have fun while you're here.
真有你的！希望你在這裡玩得愉快！

從電影對話中找靈感

▶ Want cup of coffee or a bite to eat?
想喝點咖啡或吃點東西嗎？ ·············· 高年級實習生

▶ That's a long trip. You must be hungry.
坐了這麼久的車，你一定餓了吧！ ·············· 因為愛你

▶ I just thought I'd drop by.
我順路來看看。 ·············· 與外婆同行

▶ You're a lot different than talking on the phone.
你和電話中的感覺完全不一樣。 ·············· 丹林柯林斯

▶ Let me show you the rest.
我再帶你看看其他地方。 ·············· 丹林柯林斯

▶ You surprised to see me.
你見到我很驚訝。·· 🎬◀ 全面進化

▶ Let's go for the tour.
走吧，帶你們轉轉！··· 🎬◀ 派特的幸福劇本

▶ I'll call you a cab.
我幫你叫輛車。·· 🎬◀ 與外婆同行

▶ I'll give you a ride to the hotel.
我開車送你去旅館。·· 🎬◀ 搖滾女王

▶ I am sorry for dropping in so suddenly.
抱歉這麼突然來訪。·· 🎬◀ 愛情失控點

▶ You've got all jet-lagged, have you?
你是時差沒調過來吧？··· 🎬◀ 無處可逃

▶ We'll start to wind the engines down.
我們開始慢慢地調整時差。··· 🎬◀ 無處可逃

▶ I am sure that you've has a long trip.
你肯定長途跋涉辛苦了。··· 🎬◀ 愛情失控點

▶ What hotel are you staying in right now?
你現在住在哪個飯店？··· 🎬◀ 翻轉幸福

最容易運用的職場關鍵字　**Have**

　　公司正在準備舉辦記者會，你問老闆現場需不需放置幾盆花，老闆回答：「Nice to have.」意思是有放也不錯，但如果是「非有不可；必備品」時，就應該說must-have，例如說：「It is a must-have document.」（這是非有不可的文件。）

　　Have的意思可以是「有；擁有；吃」，例如要表示吃午餐，可以說have lunch或是luncheon。Have還有做為「完成式」的用法，就是have加上過去分詞，意思是「已經；曾經」，例如have done（已經完成）。

　　Have也常放在字首，用來表示祝福，此時的have就解釋為「體驗；

經驗」，例如「Have a nice day.」（祝你有個愉快的一天）、「Have fun.」
（祝你玩得愉快），其他和have相關的用法請參閱以下例句。

1 Have aux. 已經；曾經
This is very good information. I would have thought the opposite.
這是很棒的訊息，和我想的相反。

2 Have v. 有
This will be the first time I will have the opportunity to look closely at your business.
這將是第一次我有機會仔細看看你們的業務。

3 Have to aux. 必須
I have to give Henry credit in building this team.
我必須把建立這個團隊的功勞歸功於亨利。

4 Nice to have ph. 很高興有；有很好
It's nice to have variety.
變換花樣總是好的。

百用句型

- Have a ＿＿＿＿＿＿＿＿＿＿ .
  祝你 ＿＿＿＿＿＿＿＿＿＿ 。
  ①nice trip（旅途愉快）；②safe flight（飛行平安）；
  ③nice weekend（周末愉快）

- How was your ＿＿＿＿＿＿＿＿＿＿ ?
  ＿＿＿＿＿＿＿＿＿＿ 還好嗎？
  ①travel（旅行）；②weekend（周末）；
  ③interview（面試）；④meeting（會議）

出差地的工作協助應對

　　出差若是到國外分部，可能會待在辦公室裡工作，通常同事會幫你安排一個臨時座位，但由於環境不熟悉，總會有事情需求助國外同事，例如要上網、傳真、喝水、廁所、借文具等，此時就得用上一些英文求助了。

情境模擬對話篇

A Excuse me. Can I use the fax machine?
　　對不起，我可以用一下傳真機嗎？

B Sure. Go ahead.
　　當然，請用。

A It seems doesn't work.
　　好像不能用。

B Let me check. No way. Fax went down again.
　　我看看，不會吧！傳真又掛了。

B I'll call an IT colleague to fix it. Wait a minute.
　　我打電話叫資訊部門的同事來修理。請稍等！

A Is there a bathroom I can use?
　　有洗手間能借用一下嗎？

B It's down the hall on the right.
　　就在走廊到底的右手邊。

B This works perfectly now.
現在能正常使用了。

A That's great. How do I send a fax to Taiwan?
太好了！我要如何傳真到台灣呢？

B Oh, it's an international call and you need a code. You can use mine.
喔，這是國際電話，你需要一個代碼，你可以用我的代碼。

A Thank you very much for all your help.
多謝你所有的幫忙！

B Anytime.
不客氣。

從電影對話中找靈感

▶ I'm sorry to bother you.
很抱歉打擾你。 ······ 當辣妹來敲門

▶ Can you print it?
你可以印出來嗎？ ······ 驚爆焦點

▶ Would you mind if we just use your computer for a second?
你介意我們用一下你的電腦嗎？ ······ 當辣妹來敲門

▶ This phone's supposed to work internationally.
照說這手機是全球通的。 ······ 無處可逃

▶ How can I access the internet/intranet?
我如何連上外部網路／內部網路？ ······ 安諾瑪麗莎

▶ I'd like to make an international call.
我想打國際電話。 ······ 無處可逃

▶ Where can I find the plug?
哪裡有插座？ ······ 白宮風雲

最容易運用的職場關鍵字　Work

發現某項設施故障了，想用英文表達「故障了」，很多人會直譯：「It's broken.」但這不是正確的用法，應該說：「It's not working.」。Work也常解釋成「行得通」，形容某個方法或策略有沒有效，例如說：「It doesn't work.」（這是行不通的。）

和work相關的片語中，最常使用的是work on及work out，前者的意思是「在做；從事於」，例如老闆詢問你某項工作進度如何，就可以回答：「We are working on it.」（我們正在做。）Work out的意思是「解決」，但它有另一個意思是「健身或運動」，例如：「You work out?」（你健身嗎？）

Homework一般是翻譯成學生的「家庭作業」，但在職場上，衍生的意思是「準備工作」，例如有次總部的大老闆突然要來台灣視察，台灣老闆在週五下午召集大家，討論要如何準備簡報，結束前她就說：「大家這個週末有homework要做囉！」其他和work相關的用法請參閱以下例句。

1 **Co-work** v. 一起合作
Let's co-work on this issue.
讓我們在這個議題上一起合作。

2 **Workable** adj. 可使用的；切實可行的
We find out it is not workable.
我們發現這是不可行的。

3 **Workshop** n. 研討會
We are planning a year end workshop on Dec 14th.
我們正在計畫一場12月14日的年終研討會。

3 **Framework** n. 架構
We believe this framework can help guide our frontline through 2017.
我們相信這個架構可以幫助引導我們的前線同仁穿越過2017年。

4 Network n. 社交網絡；人際關係網絡

We are the largest foreign company in this industry, with an extensive retail distribution network in Taiwan.

在這個行業裡，我們是最大的外商，在台灣有廣泛的零售分銷網絡。

百用句型

- Can I use your _____ .
  可以跟你借 _____ 嗎？

  ①bathroom（廁所）；
  ②stapler（訂書機）；
  ③printer（印表機）；
  ④phone（電話）；
  ⑤computer（電腦）

電影經典名言可以這樣應用

在職場上，同事之間若談到一些八卦，也可以用到這句話。

- **He said, she said.**
  人云亦云。

  引自《驚爆焦點》

Unit 10　出差期間的觀光旅遊

　　有機會到國外出差是很難得的機會，千萬不要只有工作或待在飯店裡，一定要找些空檔到處走走，體驗不同國家或城市的風俗民情，嚐嚐當地的小吃，此時就會用上一些日常生活的英文，例如問路、找特定景點或請求提供各種建議。

情境模擬對話篇

A Is there anything in this area worth seeing?
這附近有什麼值得去的景點嗎？

B Merlion park. You can see images of Singapore's national icon, the mythical Merlion with the head of a lion and the body of a fish.
魚尾獅公園。你能看到新加坡的國家象徵「神話魚尾獅」，它有著獅頭和魚身。

A Is it far from here?
離這裡遠嗎？

B You're fifteen minutes away. But it's peak hours now. I would suggest you take a subway.
只有十五分鐘車程。不過現在是尖峰時段，我建議你搭捷運。

A Can you direct me to the nearest MRT station?
請告訴我最近的捷運站怎麼走？

B Go straight and turn right at the second traffic light.
直走，在第二個紅綠燈右轉。

A Thank you so much.
非常感謝！

抵達景點

B Excuse me. Could you take a picture of me?
不好意思，可以幫我拍張照嗎？

A No problem. Say "cheese"！You check if it's ok.
沒問題。說「起司」！你看一下照得可以嗎？

B Perfect. Thanks
很好，謝謝！

從電影對話中找靈感

▶ Excuse me. Do you mind taking our photo?
不好意思，可以幫我們拍張照嗎？ .... 時空永恆的愛戀

▶ My feet are dying.
我的腳快斷了！ .... 當辣妹來敲門

▶ You look kind of lost.
你看起來迷路了。 .... 詭影任務

▶ Do you guys speak English?
你們會說英語嗎？ .... 白日夢冒險王

▶ I'm afraid I can't help you.
恐怕我幫不了你們。 .... 當辣妹來敲門

▶ Is there a bathroom around here?
這附近有洗手間嗎？ .... 命運鞋奏曲

▶ Let's look around.
我們四周看看。 .... 紙上城市

▶ I'm not interested.
我沒興趣。 .... 45 年

▶ It's gonna be a squeeze up there.
那裡快擠爆了！ ⋯⋯⋯⋯⋯⋯⋯⋯⋯⋯⋯⋯⋯⋯⋯⋯⋯⋯⋯⋯ 聖母峰

最容易運用的職場關鍵字 | Take

當別人問你願意花多少力量或資源完成它，若要表達決心，可以回答：「Whatever it takes.」（不計代價。）也可以翻譯成「什麼都好談」。

Take的意思有很多，可以是「拿；取；帶領；接受；花費；吃（藥）」，例如問部屬：「Can you take the lead for this project?」（你可以主導這個專案嗎？）還有吃藥不是用eat，而是take the medicine。

Take也是萬用動詞，例如take a look（看一下）、take it easy（放輕鬆）、take your time（別急；慢慢來）、take leave（休假）、take notes（做筆記）、take risks（冒風險）、take steps（採取步驟）及take the initiative（採取主動）等，其他和take相關的用法請參閱以下表格及例句。

英文	中譯	英文	中譯
Take the chance	碰運氣；冒風險	Take action	採取行動
Take into consideration	考慮到；顧及	Take into account	斟酌；考慮
Take away	拿走；帶走	Take turns	輪流

1 **Take** V. 接
Can you please take this forward?
之後可以由你接手嗎？

2 **Take in** ph. 接受；吸收
The club took in a new member last week.
俱樂部上星期又吸收了一名新會員。

3 Take on `ph.` 雇用

We're taking on 50 new staff this year.

我們今年要雇用 50 名新員工。

4 Take off `ph.` 休假

He took two weeks off in August.

他在八月份休了兩個星期的假。

5 Take place `ph.` 發生；舉行

We have to follow the strictest guidelines to ensure that governance and control take place.

我們必須遵循最嚴格的指導方針，以確保治理和控制發生。

電影經典名言可以這樣應用

　　史帝夫和昔日同事聊天時，他同事說史帝夫以前曾威脅他，史帝夫用這句話做解釋，意思是他知道同事有能力做到，才故意給他壓力。在職場上，可以運用在當你看到和自己一樣有能力的人時。

• **People are attracted to people with talent.**

有才之士惺惺相惜。　　　　　　　　　　　　　引自《史帝夫賈伯斯》

Unit 11　出差外的伴手禮採購

　　出差一定要找機會去逛當地人才會去的市集，才能吃到或買到真正道地的東西，順便帶些土產回去給家人或同事，而且價格會便宜很多。

情境模擬對話篇

A Where can I buy some local food product to take home?
我在哪裡可以買到一些土產帶回家？

B I would suggest you go to Chinatown. You can find some good and cheap local food.
我建議你去中國城。你可以找到一些好又便宜的當地美食。

商店內選購

A What do you need?
你需要什麼？

B I'll just have a look around.
我先隨便看看。

選購結束

A We'll even assemble it for you.
我們還會幫你裝好。

B That would be great.
那太好了！

A I need your personal information and shipping address. Should have been delivered this afternoon.
我需要你的個人資訊及送貨地址。今天下午應能送到。

B How much in total?
總共多少錢？

A It's $150 in total.
總共150元。

B Do you take credit cards?
你們收信用卡嗎？

A No. Cash only.
不行。只收現金。

B Gotta get an ATM. Please excuse me for a moment.
得去找台自動提款機，請稍等我一下。

A There is one around the corner.
角落那邊有一台。

從電影對話中找靈感

▶ That makes it all worthwhile.
物超所值。 ································· 🎥 聖母峰

▶ I'll take this one.
我要這個了。 ································· 🎥 搖滾女王

▶ Do you want me to google how much this is worth on eBay?
要不要我在谷歌上搜尋一下在eBay上賣多少錢？ ········· 🎥 與外婆同行

▶ Do you have any newspaper in English?
你們有英文的報紙嗎？ ····················· 🎥 無處可逃

▶ It's just a couple of hours from here.
離這裡只有幾小時車程。 ··················· 🎥 時空永恆的愛戀

▶ Just a few minutes away.
就在附近。 ······························ 🎥 實習大叔

▶ Thank you very much for bringing me here.
謝謝你帶我來這裡。 ······················· 🎥 機械姬

▶ I'll have a regular with blueberries and coconut please.
麻煩我要一個一般大小的藍莓及椰子口味。………… 🎥 我想念我自己

▶ There you go. There's your receipt.
好了，這是你的收據。……………………………………… 🎥 搖滾女王

▶ I'm afraid we're out of stock.
恐怕我們賣完了。………………………………………… 🎥 因為愛你

▶ Sorry, no smoking on the floor.
不好意思，這層樓不能抽菸。…………………………… 🎥 因為愛你

最容易運用的職場關鍵字 | Look

　　Look常用在一般對話中，當你要別人注意聽或有點情緒時，就會說：「Look.」（聽好。）還有當別人向你徵詢意見時，就可以回覆：「Looks good.」（看起來還不錯）、「Looks OK.」（看起來可以）。

　　當你要求別人看一下郵件或文件，可以說：「Please take a look.」還有當別人用奇怪的眼光看你時，你也可以說：「Don't give me that look.」（別那麼看我。）

　　Look for的意思是「尋找」，例如：「I don't think this is what I am looking for.」（我不認為這是我所期待的。）Look like的意思是「看起來像是」，例如：「What does it look like?」（它看起來像什麼呢？）Look forward to的意思是「期待」，例如「I look forward to hearing more good news from you.」（我期待著聽到你更多的好消息。）

　　衍生字outlook的意思是「觀點；看法；展望；前景」，例如Global economic outlook（全球經濟展望。）Investment outlook（投資展望）。Overlook的意思「忽視；沒注意到」，例如「I might be willing to overlook that.」（我想我能忽略這點），在職場上也常解釋成「監督；監視」，其他和look相關的用法請參閱以下例句。

1 Look n. 看

Can you take a look and get back to me by end of tomorrow please?

可以請你看一下，並且在明天下班前回覆我嗎？

2 Look into ph. 檢查；研究

Not sure of all the facts, but can you help look into it?

不確認所有的事實，但你可以幫忙檢查一下嗎？

3 Look through ph. 徹底審查

Stella has looked through the agreement and generally it's OK.

史黛拉已徹底審查協議書，大體上來說它是沒問題的。

解答／十句常用出差英文的英譯

1. Are you going a business trip?
2. What time we heading out?
3. What's the actual flying time from here to Chicago?
4. I can tell by your accent.
5. Do you have chang for $100?
6. I have a reservation under Kevin Yang.
7. Can I get a free map of this city?
8. Jesus, how long has it been?
9. Is there a bathroom I can use?
10. Is there anything in this area worth seeing?

第 **5** 章

合作溝通不可少的應對用語

試試看下列幾句常用的職場應對短句，如何用英文表達？

1. 下次盡量不要再犯了。
2. 我立刻去辦。
3. 今天我想和他談五分鐘。
4. 我會搞定他，只是要更多時間。
5. 是我考慮不周。
6. 別小看自己。
7. 你的報告做得很好。
8. 把這事搞定。
9. 你可以跟我說實話嗎？
10.我們的默契不錯！

（答案在本章最後一頁）

Unit 1 上班遲到的應對進退

　　上班難免遇到遲到的狀況，以下是以「睡過頭」為例，當然這不是好的理由，除非你前一天是因為熬夜加班。通常比較好的理由是：身體不舒服、小孩有狀況或其他突發狀況如交通工具故障、車禍等。

情境模擬對話篇

B Hey, you all right?
嘿，你還好嗎？

A Oh, I'm sorry, I overslept.
喔，抱歉！我睡過頭了。

B Okay, well, you had a client waiting for you. Luckily, Jack here covered for you.
好吧！有客戶等著見你了。很幸運，傑克幫你掩護過去了。

A Well, I'm sorry. Thank you.
很抱歉，多謝了！

B Let's try not to let it happen again.
下次盡量不要再犯了。

A You got it. Of course.
聽你的，一定。

B It's not like you, anyway.
這有點不像你的風格。

A Yeah.
是啊！

B Hey, are you ok?
嘿，你還好嗎？

A I'm sorry, I was not feeling very well this morning.
很抱歉，今早我感覺不太舒服。

B You should take the day off and feel better, okay?
你應該請假，讓自己舒服些，好嗎？

A I've got a lot of ground to cover.
我還有很多事要處理。

B Don't push yourself too hard.
別太勉強自己。

A It's okay. I'm just got a little dizzy right now.
還好啦！我現在只是有點頭暈。

B Need any help?
需要幫忙嗎？

A Thanks, boss. I can handle it.
謝謝老闆！我能搞定的。

從電影對話中找靈感

▶ I apologize for the trouble I have caused you.
抱歉給您帶來困擾。 ······················· 📹 拍賣家

▶ I had a personal thing this afternoon.
我下午有私事。 ····························· 📹 大賣空

▶ That has to be the worst excuse I've ever heard.
這是我聽過最差勁的藉口。 ················· 📹 心靈大道

▶ It won't happen again.
下不為例。 ································· 📹 心靈大道

▶ Could I get away early?
我可以提早離開嗎？ ······················· 📹 詭影任務

▶ You're not supposed to be working today.
你今天不應該上班的。·······························📹◀ 與外婆同行

換種說法也可通

各種不舒服的說法
1	I'm not feeling so well today. 我今天覺得不太舒服。《驚天換日》
2	I feel very achy. 我覺得不舒服。《愛情失控點》
3	Like maybe I'm coming down with something. 可能是我生病了吧！《愛情失控點》
4	It's just a little touch of Delhi／Buddha belly. 只是有點小拉肚子。《聖母峰》
5	My stomach hurts. 我胃疼！《安諾瑪麗莎》
6	I'm actually not feeling so hot. 我真的感覺不舒服。《高年級實習生》

最容易運用的職場關鍵字 Cover

　　在電影槍戰情節中，A戰友告訴B戰友：「I cover you.」（我掩護你）；或在上班時間，同事想出去溜達一下，你也可以說：「Go ahead! I cover you.」（去吧！我掩護你／我頂替你。）電影《高年級實習生》中有句台詞：「I'm happy to cover for Mike.」（我很樂意幫邁克代班。）

　　Cover做為動詞的意思是「遮蓋；掩護；包含；涉及」，例如：「I would have had time to cover that.」（我就有時間去含蓋那部份了。）Cover做為名詞的意思是「封面；蓋子」。例如雜誌的cover story（封面故事）。電影《搖滾女王》中也有句台詞：「That was my cover story in college.」（那是我在大學時的重要事蹟。）

　　與cover相關的片語有cover up（掩飾錯誤）及cover in（完全掩

蓋），英國偶像團體「One Direction」有首歌曲叫《What makes you beautiful》，歌詞中有一句：「Don't need makeup to cover up.」（不需要化妝來掩飾。）

由cover所衍生出來的字有coverage，意思是「覆蓋範圍或媒體報導」，例如market coverage（市場覆蓋）、media coverage（媒體報導）及building coverage ratio（建蔽率）等，其他和cover相關的用法請參閱以下例句。

1 **Cover** **v.** 包含；涉及
There is some material we haven't covered yet.
有些資料我們還沒涉及到。

2 **Cover up** **ph.** 掩飾錯誤（或非法的事物等）
The government is trying to cover up the scandal.
政府企圖掩飾這件醜聞。

3 **Cover in** **ph.** 蓋住（填滿）
The car park is covered in, to keep my car dry.
停車場加了頂蓋，使我的轎車免遭雨雪。

4 **Coverage** **n.** 覆蓋範圍；媒體報導
The press conference got massive media coverage.
記者會得到媒體的廣泛報導。

Unit 2 做錯事的應對技巧

　　台灣員工犯錯時，最常有兩種反應，一是悶不吭聲，二是解釋一大堆理由，加上英文不夠好，更容易讓外籍老闆火冒三丈，其實只要簡單地回應，讓他無法繼續罵你，然後趕快去把事情搞清楚，以最快的速度回覆就行了。

情境模擬對話篇

A Hey, you alienated the customer.
嘿，你讓顧客不開心了。

B Sorry, I didn't notice it.
抱歉，我沒注意到。

A I need you to satisfy and delight the customer.
我要你滿足及討好顧客。

B Okay. I'm sorry, boss.
好的，抱歉，老闆！

A No, it's okay. Just remember, gratitude.
沒關係，只要記住，心懷感激！

B I got it. Thanks.
我知道了，謝謝！

從電影對話中找靈感

▶ I'll do it.
我會照辦。 ································· 丹麥女孩

▶ I'm on it.
我這就去辦。 ··· 🎥 通靈神探

▶ I'm working on it.
我正在做／處理。 ··· 🎥 驚爆焦點

▶ I'm taking care of that.
我來安排。 ··· 🎥 全面進化

▶ We're working it out.
我們正在解決。 ··· 🎥 派特的幸福劇本

▶ I'll get on it right away.
我立刻去辦。 ··· 🎥 安諾瑪麗莎

▶ I'm formulating a plan.
我正在想辦法。 ··· 🎥 白宮風雲

▶ We are fixing it.
我們正在補救。 ··· 🎥 白宮風雲

▶ We are underway.
我們在執行中。 ··· 🎥 白宮風雲

▶ We are looking into it.
我們正在調查。 ··· 🎥 白宮風雲

▶ I am checking it out.
我正在查。 ··· 🎥 白宮風雲

▶ Right away.
馬上好。 ··· 🎥 大賣空

▶ I shall fix anything.
我會處理好所有事。 ··· 🎥 大夢想家

▶ I'll work my hardest.
我會盡全力。 ··· 🎥 實習大叔

最容易運用的職場關鍵字 | Make

在職場上，主管勉勵部屬或團隊時，經常會說：「We're going to make it.」（我們會成功的。）

Make這個字簡單又實用，意思可以是「使；做；製造；獲得；成為；使成功」等，例如「When do we need to make this effective?」（什麼時候我們需要讓它生效呢？）

與make相關的片語也很多，包括make sense（有道理）及make it（成功；趕上；做或完成某事）等，例如你在安排會議，詢問某人這個時間行不行，就問：「Can you make it at 2pm?」（下午兩點你可以嗎？）其他與make相關的片語如下：

英文	中譯	英文	中譯
Make it clear	說清楚	Make it happen	使它發生
Make a joke	開玩笑	Make a decision	做決策
Make a mistake	犯錯	Make a recommendation	做建議
Make friends	交朋友	Make an announcement	公布
Make promise	承諾	Make a nomination	提名
Make up	編造；補足	Make sure	確定
Make believe	假裝	Make oneself at home	不要拘束

由make所衍生出來的字有Tailor-made（量身訂作的；特製的），常用在公司為VIP客戶量身訂作商品或服務，其他和make相關的用法請參閱以下例句。

1 Make v. 使；讓

Can you make this announcement more interesting, more marketing oriented?
你能讓這公告更有趣、更市場導向嗎？

2 **Make the call** ph. 做裁決
I have left them to make the final call.
我已經留給他們做最後的決定。

3 **Tailor-made** adj. 量身訂作的；特製的
The job is tailor-made for him.
這工作是為他量身訂作的。

4 **Make use of** ph. 使用
Please make use of the attached cover sheet template for the paper submission.
繳交文件時請使用附件的封面範本。

電影經典名言可以這樣應用

在職場上，奉勸別人要抓大方向，不要著墨於細節時，就可以說這句話。

- **The trick is not to examine things too closely.**
  秘訣是看事情不要太鑽牛角尖。　　　　　　　　　引自《愛情失控點》

Unit 3 | 跟祕書預約老闆的開會時間

　　祕書具有極大的影響力，因為他知道老闆的行程、能決定與老闆會面的優先順序、知道老闆的喜怒哀樂，所以和祕書套好交情很重要。

情境模擬對話篇

A Hey, Cathy. Is boss around?
嘿，凱西，老闆在嗎？

B He's right in here. But he's expecting a conference call.
他就在裡面，但是他在等一個電話會議。

A I want five minutes of his time today.
今天我想和他談五分鐘。

B Okay, I have secured an appointment for you today at 4:55 p.m. Please be prompt.
好的，我給你預約了今天下午四點五十五分，請準時。

A Thanks. How's his mood today?
謝了！他今天心情如何？

B He's been in such a touchy mood.
他最近情緒好敏感。

A Something big going on recently?
最近有什麼大事嗎？

B I'm really not at liberty to say.
我真的不能說。

A What the hell do you know?
你到底知道什麼？

B Go be curious somewhere else. I got work to do.
去別處好奇！我還要工作。

A Fine. Talk to you later.
好吧！晚點再聊！

從電影對話中找靈感

▶ I'd like to speak with Thomas.
我想找湯瑪士談談。 .... 🎬 驚爆焦點

▶ Any tips before I go in?
在我進去前給點提示吧！ .... 🎬 高年級實習生

▶ I set you up with a face-to-face.
我給你安排見面的機會。 .... 🎬 大賣空

▶ Just confirm something for me, okay?
就幫我確認一下，可以嗎？ .... 🎬 史帝夫賈伯斯

▶ What do you have to report?
你有什麼要報告的？ .... 🎬 機械姬

▶ My secretary will contact you the date and details.
我的祕書會通知你日期和細節。 .... 🎬 心靈大道

▶ Can you get us some coffee?
你能拿咖啡來嗎？ .... 🎬 心靈捕手

▶ You got 30 seconds. Make your case.
給你三十秒，快說吧！ .... 🎬 搖搖欲墜

▶ Please be patient.
請耐心等候！ .... 🎬 翻轉幸福

▶ Go right ahead.
直接進去吧！ .... 🎬 謎樣的雙眼

▶ Look like you're gonna be here a while.
看來你還得在這裡待一會。 .... 🎬 高年級實習生

▶ Should I tell them you'll be late?
我該對他們說你會晚一點嗎？ ·············· 🎥◀ 謎樣的雙眼

最容易運用的職場關鍵字 | Conference

　　開會形式除了面對面之外，為了加強效率或克服距離的問題，衍生出 conference call（電話會議）、video conference（視訊會議），其中電話會議常被簡稱為concall。有時也會看到有人使用teleconference，泛指使用電話及電視的電信會議，可以包含前述兩者。

　　隨著網路普及化，有時候大家乾脆就在自己的位子上對著電腦的 webcam開會，稱為web conference（網路會議）。

　　Conference的意思是「正式會議；討論會；協商會」，和meeting有些差異。一般來說，meeting比較沒那麼正式，參與的人數比較少，而conference相對正式，有一個特定的議程，參與的人可能屬於不同背景，共同討論一個關心的主題。

　　此外，meeting多半在公司內部，而conference則可能是承租飯店的會議室或教育訓練中心。前述所及的電話會議或視訊會議，雖然是conference衍生出來的用法，但多半是在公司內部舉行。

　　還有一個很常用的詞是press conference（記者會），press的意思是「報刊；新聞界；記者們」，而press release就是「新聞稿」。其他和conference相關的用法請參閱以下例句。

1 Conference n. 正式會議
I will be traveling from Tue. to Fri. to a Group conference in Singapore.
我將從週二到週五前往新加坡參加一個集團的會議。

2 Conference call ph. 電話會議
A follow-up conference call was arranged today with Adam on the approval of the product.
關於這項產品的核准，一個與亞當的後續電話會議將被安排在今天。

3 Video conference `ph.` 視訊會議

Bill's Chicago office uses video conferenc to communicate with the New York affiliates.

比爾在芝加哥的辦公室，使用視訊會議和在紐約的分公司進行溝通。

4 Press conference `ph.` 記者會

We have prepared the press release to be given to journalists at press conference.

我們已經準備好新聞稿要給在記者會的記者。

電影經典名言可以這樣應用

　　這句話常用在追求異性時，對方明明是有意思，但卻故意刁難，想讓對方感受沒那麼容易得手。或是也可以用在談判過程中。

• **You keep playing hard to get.**
你繼續欲擒故縱。　　　　　　　　　　　　　　　　引自《實習大叔》

Unit 4　面對主管詢問的應對進退

　　面對老闆的詢問，能否回答適切，關鍵就在於是否能聽懂問題，所以要先熟悉外籍老闆常問的問題，同時也要理解如何回答比較好。

主管常用的問話語句

▶ How's the investigation going?
　調查得如何？ ………………………………………… 🎥 通靈神探

▶ Where have you been?
　你去哪兒了？ ………………………………………… 🎥 偷書賊

▶ What are you going to do now?
　你現在打算怎麼做？ ………………………………… 🎥 白宮風雲

▶ Exactly how long is this going to take?
　這要弄多久？ ………………………………………… 🎥 翻轉幸福

▶ What are you working on now?
　你們現在在做什麼？ ………………………………… 🎥 驚爆焦點

▶ What's he here for?
　他來做什麼？ ………………………………………… 🎥 翻轉幸福

▶ Can you get to him?
　你能聯繫上他嗎？ …………………………………… 🎥 驚爆焦點

▶ Have you met this guy in person yet?
　你和他見過面嗎？ …………………………………… 🎥 驚爆焦點

▶ What on earth are you talking about?
　你到底在講什麼？ …………………………………… 🎥 心靈捕手

▶ What took you so long?
　你為什麼這麼久才行動？ …………………………… 🎥 驚爆焦點

▶ What the hell is going on?
到底是怎麼回事？ ················· 🎥 《大賣空》

▶ What's this all about?
到底是怎麼回事？ ················· 🎥 大夢想家

▶ What can I get you?
你要什麼？ ························· 🎥 天菜大廚

▶ What's it say?
裡面怎麼說的？ ··················· 🎥 心靈捕手

▶ What have you got?
你找到什麼？ ····················· 🎥 驚爆焦點

▶ Why don't we just get it out of the way now?
為何不現在就解決？ ··············· 🎥 心靈捕手

▶ Why aren't there any records?
為什麼沒有任何紀錄？ ············· 🎥 驚爆焦點

▶ When is this?
何時的事？ ························· 🎥 心靈捕手

▶ When are you done with those meetings?
何時能完成那些會談？ ············· 🎥 心靈捕手

▶ Where does this leave us?
這能帶給我什麼結果？ ············· 🎥 凸槌三人行

▶ Who's your source?
來源是哪？ ························· 🎥 驚爆焦點

▶ How long ago was that?
那是多久以前？ ··················· 🎥 白日夢冒險王

▶ How did it go?
情況怎麼樣／進展如何？ ··········· 🎥 機械姬

▶ How did that happen?
怎麼會發生？ ····················· 🎥 機械姬

▶ How much longer do you need to get through these clips?
你需要多長時間才能查完這些剪報？ ··· 🎥 驚爆焦點

部屬可以應用的語句

▶ It's improving.
有進展。 ··· 🎥 通靈神探

▶ I'll get him. I just need more time.
我會搞定他，只是要更多時間。 ··········· 🎥 驚爆焦點

▶ It shouldn't take more than a day
應該不超過一天。 ······························· 🎥 翻轉幸福

▶ We're really just trolling around for our next story.
我們正四處探尋下一個題材。 ············· 🎥 驚爆焦點

▶ I'll try.
我會試。 ··· 🎥 白宮風雲

百用句型

• What the hell are you _____ ?
你到底在 _____ 什麼？
①thinking（想）；
②doing（做）；
③talking about（說）；
④waiting for（等）；
⑤looking at（看）

最容易運用的職場關鍵字　**Product**

Product是每家公司的核心，這個字在商用英文中必然經常出現，例如product introduction（產品簡介）、product training（產品訓練）、product design（產品設計）、product launch（產品發行）等。在電影《翻轉幸福》中有句台詞：「I sell product affordably, but I don't sell cheap product.」（我賣人們負擔得起的產品，但我不賣便宜貨。）

Productivity的意思是「生產力；產能」，表示人力或機器所能創造的產能，例如：「經過一連串的教育訓練，業務同仁在這一季的productivity已大幅提升了。」

Production的意思是「生產；量產」，當一個產品經過設計、測試、非正式上市（soft launch），一切都就緒後，就會開始進入production的階段。Produce做為動詞的意思是「生產；製造；創造」，做為名詞意思是「農產品」。

在職場上常聽到的職稱PM，代表product manager（產品經理）或project manager（專案經理）。Product line的意思是「產品線」，例如Samsung在手機部門的product line共有五項商品，又例如：「和主要競爭者比較，我們的product line稍嫌不足。」其他和product相關的用法請參閱以下例句。

1 Product n. 產品；產物
You have my approval to proceed with this product as discussed over the past few days.
如同過去幾天的討論，我同意繼續進行這項產品。

2 Productivity n. 生產力
Attrition is still an issue and contributed to lower productivity.
人員耗損（離職）仍然是一個問題，並導致生產力降低。

3 Production n. 生產；量產
Before the deployment in production, we need your support to confirm the below announcement.
在開始生產之前，我們需要你的協助來確認以下的公告。

Unit 5　被主管責罵的應對會話

在西方文化中，不要輕易說抱歉，因為對方會認為你真的錯了，但面對老闆，若真的是做錯了，就趕緊認錯，繼續狡辯可能會被罵得更慘。

主管常用的不滿語句

▶ Do I make myself clear?
你聽清楚了嗎？ ……………………………………………… 🎥 白宮風雲

▶ I'm deeply disappointed in you.
我對你很失望。 ……………………………………………… 🎥 與外婆同行

▶ Why you thought that was a good idea?
你為何認為這是好主意？ ……………………………………… 🎥 出棋制勝

▶ There are no accidents.
這一切都不是意外。 …………………………………………… 🎥 因為愛你

▶ You really giving me a headache right now.
你現在真的讓我很頭疼。 ……………………………………… 🎥 宵禁

▶ It was entirely predictable.
根本是可預見的。 ……………………………………………… 🎥 詭影任務

▶ Did I ask you to do that?
我讓你這麼做了嗎？ …………………………………………… 🎥 白宮風雲

▶ It's the dumbest thing I've heard it.
這是我聽過最傻的事。 ………………………………………… 🎥 宵禁

▶ I don't think you're seeing what I need.
你似乎不明白我需要什麼。 …………………………………… 🎥 白日夢冒險王

▶ I just hope you heard what I said.
我希望你聽懂我說的話了。 ······································· 派特的幸福劇本

▶ How many more ways can you guys screw this thing up?
你們還有多少紕漏可以出？ ······································· 白宮末日

▶ Don't ever do it again.
別再做出這種事了。 ·· 白宮風雲

▶ Have you lost your mind?
你神智不清嗎？ ·· 白宮風雲

▶ You guys should know better.
你們太不懂事了。 ·· 丹林柯林斯

▶ You'll give me a heart attack.
你會讓我得心臟病的。 ·· 丹林柯林斯

▶ It's no excuse.
沒有藉口。 ··· 丹林柯林斯

▶ This is not open for discussion.
這沒什麼可商量的。 ·· 丹林柯林斯

▶ Save your breath.
不用說了。 ··· 非禮勿弒

▶ I'm hoping for a better answer than that.
這個答案實在不夠好。 ·· 謎樣的雙眼

▶ You always were a little slow.
你一直都有點遲鈍。 ·· 謎樣的雙眼

▶ You don't get to talk back.
你不要回嘴。 ··· 天菜大廚

部屬可以應用的語句

▶ I see what you're seeing.
我懂你的意思。 ·· 白宮風雲

▶ I'm terribly sorry to disappoint you.
很抱歉讓你失望了。 ··· 🎥 實習大叔

▶ I'm not clear headed.
我沒想清楚。 ··· 🎥 宵禁

▶ It was kind of fault.
是我太大意。 ··· 🎥 宵禁

▶ I'm terribly sorry.
我很抱歉。 ··· 🎥 實習大叔

▶ I misjudged that.
我判斷錯了。 ··· 🎥 搖搖欲墜

▶ I'm thinking straight.
是我考慮不周。 ·· 🎥 安諾瑪麗莎

▶ It's on me.
都怪我。 ··· 🎥 謎樣的雙眼

▶ I will make adjustments.
我會調整。 ··· 🎥 我想念我自己

▶ It's not gonna be like last time.
這次不會像上次那樣。 ··· 🎥 白宮風雲

▶ I'm almost done here.
我馬上就好。 ··· 🎥 白宮風雲

▶ We are looking into it.
我們正在調查。 ·· 🎥 白宮風雲

▶ We got a pattern.
我們找到一個模式了。 ··· 🎥 加州大地震

▶ I'm ready for my next assignment.
我準備好接下個任務了。 ·· 🎥 搖搖欲墜

▶ We double-checked.
我們再次確認過了。 ·· 🎥 加州大地震

▶ We're keeping an eye on it.
我們會注意。 ⋯⋯⋯⋯⋯⋯⋯⋯⋯⋯⋯⋯⋯⋯⋯⋯ 🎥聖母峰

▶ It's here. I've been taking notes.
在這裡，我都記下來了。 ⋯⋯⋯⋯⋯⋯⋯⋯⋯⋯⋯ 🎥丹林柯林斯

▶ I'm getting it.
我開始上手了。 ⋯⋯⋯⋯⋯⋯⋯⋯⋯⋯⋯⋯⋯⋯⋯ 🎥實習大叔

▶ It's more than I deserve.
這多於我應得的。 ⋯⋯⋯⋯⋯⋯⋯⋯⋯⋯⋯⋯⋯⋯⋯ 🎥偷書賊

▶ I always like a challenge.
我一向喜歡挑戰。 ⋯⋯⋯⋯⋯⋯⋯⋯⋯⋯⋯⋯⋯⋯⋯ 🎥全面進化

▶ I apologize if I overstepped in some way.
如果我在某方面越界了，我向你道歉。 ⋯⋯⋯⋯⋯⋯ 🎥高年級實習生

最容易運用的職場關鍵字　Clear

　　電影《變身》的劇情中，有一段描述從國外留學回來的電視台總經理嚴厲地訓斥員工後說了一句：「Am I clear?」，於是A員工就問B員工：「這句英文是什麼意思？」B員工回答：「我乾淨嗎？」引發哄堂大笑。

　　這句話在職場上經常使用，意思是「我說得夠清楚嗎？」或「你明白嗎？」例如當你報告完一件事情後，不那麼確定大家是否了解，就可以這麼問。這句話也經常用在主管生氣時對部屬警告，意思是「你們都給我聽清楚了」。

　　Clear這個字可以做為動詞、形容詞及副詞，分別的意思為「清除」、「清楚的」、「清晰地」，例如在電影《史帝夫賈伯斯》中有句台詞：「I came here to clear the air.」（我是來消除誤會的。）

　　其他和clear相關的用法請參閱以下例句。

1 Clear V. 清除
I need to clear my head.
我需要排除雜念。

2 Clear adj. 清楚的
Hope my position is clear.
希望我的立場是清楚的。

3 Unclear adj. 不清楚的
I am afraid the above is still very unclear.
恐怕上述還是很不清楚。

4 Clear up ph. 清理
That clears things up.
這樣就解釋清楚了。

電影經典名言可以這樣應用

　　主角在高齡退休後，想再重新回到職場，他在自製面試影片時，想說服雇主，雖然自己年紀大但仍有工作熱情，便以這句名言當例子。

• **Musicians don't retire. They stop when there's no more music in them.**
音樂家不退休，當他們心中再沒有音樂時才會收手。

引自《高年級實習生》

Unit 6　鼓勵／稱讚同事的應用會話

在西方文化中，鼓勵及稱讚部屬是主管重要的職責之一，學學電影中的台詞怎麼說？

從電影對話中找靈感

▶ Not saying that couldn't.
不要說做不到。 …………………………………… 🎥 搖搖欲墜

▶ Don't underestimate yourself.
別小看自己。 …………………………………… 🎥 全面進化

▶ Try to stay positive.
試著保持正面思考。 …………………………… 🎥 派特的幸福劇本

▶ You gotta have faith.
你要有信心。 …………………………………… 🎥 派特的幸福劇本

▶ You'll have my full support.
你會得到我全力的支持。 ……………………… 🎥 空中救援

▶ Don't stress.
不要有壓力。 …………………………………… 🎥 當辣妹來敲門

▶ Everything will work out for us.
一切都會好起來的。 …………………………… 🎥 丹麥女孩

▶ One step at a time.
一步一步來。 …………………………………… 🎥 丹麥女孩

▶ Everything will be all right.
一切都會沒事的。 ……………………………… 🎥 丹麥女孩

▶ This is showing real progress.
比以前有所進步了。 …………………………… 🎥 家有兩個爸

▶ Let's look forward.
讓我們向前看。 ··· 謎樣的雙眼

▶ We need to move on.
我們要往前走。 ··· 翻轉幸福

▶ Let's make it happen.
讓我們做到。 ··· 高年級實習生

▶ Let's keep it that way.
我們繼續保持那樣。 ··· 驚爆焦點

▶ Let's get through this stuff.
讓我們克服難關。 ··· 高年級實習生

▶ Let's do it together.
讓我們一起努力。 ··· 高年級實習生

▶ Try to be open.
試著去接納。 ··· 高年級實習生

▶ We are keeping together on this.
我們要一條心。 ··· 弒訊

▶ It's impressive work.
做得很好。 ··· 詭影任務

▶ You are a resourceful guy.
你很會應變。 ··· 空中救援

▶ Great team spirit.
很好的團隊精神。 ··· 凸槌三人行

▶ You've been working really hard.
你一直很努力。 ··· 凸槌三人行

▶ You do seize the moment.
你很會把握時機嘛！ ··· 白宮風雲

▶ You did a good job with your reports.
你的報告做得很好。 ··· 凸槌三人行

▶ Nice touch.
說得很好！ ··· 凸槌三人行

最容易運用的職場關鍵字　Pick

在中文裡，我們常用「機車」形容某同事或主管不好相處，有人就譯成 motorcycle，雖然台灣人都聽得懂，但老外肯定聽不懂，而且這絕對是錯誤的英文用法，正確的用字是 picky。它是由 pick（挑選）這個字衍生而來的，什麼事都東挑西選，這個人當然就很 picky，也就是很「吹毛求疵的；挑剔的」的意思。例如「我老闆超 picky，一份報告沒被退回三、四次，是不可能過關的。」

Pick 做為動詞的意思是「選擇；挑選」，例如：「That's why I picked you.」（所以我才挑中你。）還有「挖鼻孔」也是用這個字，叫做 pick your nose。Pick 做為名詞的意思也是「選擇；挑選」，例如《空中英語雜誌》有個單元叫「Editor's Pick」，字面上的意思是「編輯挑選」，衍生之意便是「編輯推薦」。還有彈吉他的人都知道，用來刷和弦或撥弦的工具，就叫做 pick。

Pick up 意思是「拾起；搭載；接」，例如「I'll pick you up.」（我會去載你。）在口語英文中，pick up 也可以解釋為「泡妞」，例如在電影《空中救援》中有句台詞：「Is that how older men pick up younger women?」（大叔都是這樣把妹的嗎？）其他和 pick 相關的用法請參閱以下例句。

---

1 **Pick** v. 選擇；挑選
Would you consider picking this one?
你會考慮選擇這個嗎？

---

2 **Pick up** ph. 搭載；接
I insist my driver pick you up from your hotel.
我堅持派司機去飯店接你。

---

3 **Pick at** ph. 找碴；挑毛病
Why are you always picking at me?
你為什麼老是挑我的毛病？

---

4 Picky adj. 吹毛求疵的；挑剔的
I hate female boss, they are so picky.
我討厭女性上司，她們太吹毛求疵了。

換種說法也可通

中譯	常用說法	另類說法
你太過謙虛。	You are too modest.	You lack arrogance. 《天菜大廚》
記住我的話。	Remember what I said.	Mark my words. 《驚爆焦點》

電影經典名言可以這樣應用

在職場上，當工作時遇到困難，某個人的加入或協助，能讓事情繼續進行或完成，就可以這麼說。

• **Wind's from the east.**
東風來了！

引自《大夢想家》

Unit 7　提醒部屬的應對進退

當主管需要提醒或命令部屬做某些事，學學電影中的台詞怎麼說？

從電影對話中找靈感

▶ Stay focused.
保持專心！ ……………………………………… 📹 派特的幸福劇本

▶ You'll have to get used to it.
你必須習慣它。 ……………………………………… 📹 丹麥女孩

▶ We gotta keep it quiet.
這種事不能聲張。 ……………………………………… 📹 謎樣的雙眼

▶ The mouth on it.
別多嘴！ ……………………………………………… 📹 偷書賊

▶ With that in mind.
請記住這一點！ ……………………………………… 📹 白宮風雲

▶ Make it a good one.
給我好的。 …………………………………………… 📹 搖搖欲墜

▶ Get me some solid.
給我些真憑實據。 ……………………………… 📹 驚爆焦點

▶ Step it up.
加快腳步。 …………………………………………… 📹 詭影任務

▶ Figured it out.
快想出辦法。 ………………………………………… 📹 空中救援

▶ Whatever it takes.
不計代價。 …………………………………………… 📹 空中救援

▶ Make this work.
把這事搞定。 ··· 白宮風雲

▶ Pick it up again.
趕快補救。 ·· 白宮風雲

▶ Just do what I said.
照我說的做！ ·· 命運鞋奏曲

▶ You're going to fix it, now.
你去處理好，馬上。 ······································· 史帝夫賈伯斯

▶ I want to know how it went.
我想知道事情的經過。 ···································· 翻轉幸福

▶ Do a background check on him.
調查一下他的背景。 ······································· 驚爆焦點

▶ We should set that aside for now.
那件事我們現在暫且擱置吧！ ·························· 驚爆焦點

▶ Because you have to set the tone.
因為你得起表率作用。 ···································· 實習大叔

▶ Keep Josh in the loop on this.
讓喬許充分掌握這件事的狀況。 ····················· 白宮風雲

▶ There is no margin for error on this one.
這事由不得半點差錯。 ···································· 命運鞋奏曲

▶ Let me know if there is any discrepancy.
如果有不一致讓我知道。 ································· 驚天換日

▶ Bring me anything you come across.
給我所有你所發現的。 ···································· 通靈神探

▶ To figure out if this is a deal of a lifetime.
搞清楚這是不是千載難逢的好機會。 ··············· 大賣空

▶ I don't want us chasing our tails on this.
我不想我們在這上面浪費時間。 ····················· 驚爆焦點

▶ I need you to take me through the events from the beginning.
我需要你從頭跟我說明這件事的始末。 ·················· 📹◀ 空中救援

▶ It's for me to set the sample for the rest of the team.
這是讓我給其他團隊的人做表率。 ·················· 📹◀ 空中救援

▶ I insist you spend a minimum amount of time on it.
我堅持你必須盡快完成它。 ·················· 📹◀ 搖搖欲墜

▶ You need to be there by 9:30, not a minute later.
你要在九點半之前到，一分鐘也不能遲到。 ·················· 📹◀ 人質

▶ Don't screw up the most lucrative partnership this company has.
別搞砸了公司最賺錢的伙伴。 ·················· 📹◀ 詭影任務

最容易運用的職場關鍵字 **Stay**

　　Stay 做為名詞時的意思是「停留；逗留」，例如這幾年旅遊開始流行 long stay，不再是逗留幾天走馬看花，而是住上數個月，好好深入體會當地的風俗民情。

　　Stay 做為動詞，除了做為「停留」，還可解釋成「繼續；保持；堅持；停下」等，例如：「This stays between us.」（不能讓其他人知道。）Stay 後面加上形容詞也是常用的用法，例如有次部門在一週內有兩個同事提出辭呈，我寫 email 告訴老闆，老闆回覆：「Stay cool. Nothing we cannot handle.」（保持冷靜，沒有什麼事我們不能處理的。）

　　Stay away from 的意思「保持距離；不打擾」，例如職場上有些小人，表面上和你很要好，當你對他掏心掏肺，甚至在他面前抱怨主管，最後他跑去和老闆打小報告，這種人就要「Stay away from him.」（遠離他），其他和 stay 相關的用法請參閱以下例句。

1 Stay **v.** 保持

We have group audit next week. Very important we stay alert and ensure order in our shop.
我們下週有總部稽核。非常重要的是我們要保持警覺，並確保在我們這

邊的狀況良好。

2 Stay v. 保持

Given the impending typhoon, please do not stay late today and encourage your teams to leave the office before 7pm as well.

考慮到即將到來的颱風，今天請不要留到很晚，也請鼓勵你們的團隊在晚上七點前離開辦公室。

3 Stay up ph. 熬夜

John stayed up all night working.

約翰整晚熬夜工作。

4 Stay away from ph. 遠離

Suggest you to stay away from her since she is so mean.

建議你離她遠一點，因為她很卑鄙。

電影經典名言可以這樣應用

　　在職場上，若部屬為自己錯誤的行為辯護時，主管就可以說這句話教訓他。

• **One incident can change a lifetime.**
　一次事件就能改變一生。　　　　　　　　引自《派特的幸福劇本》

Unit 8　簡單扼要的適當提問

　　提問是英文對話中非常重要的環節，若不會提問，對話可能很快就會結束。通常提問句子不用長，太長反而聽不清楚，六個字以內較合適。

簡短提問語句

英文	中譯	英文	中譯
二字問句			
Really works?	真的有用？	Any news?	有什麼新鮮事？
What conditions?	什麼條件？	How so?	此話怎講？
三字問句			
Is that true?	是真的嗎？	Wasn't that strange?	那不是很奇怪嗎？
How was it?	還順利嗎？	Is that difficult?	那很難嗎？
Heard from who?	聽誰說的？	Relative to what?	從哪看出來？
What's she like?	她是怎麼樣的人？	Wasn't that bad?	還不錯吧？
Was this better?	這有比較好嗎？	What just happened?	剛才發生什麼事？
It still works?	還能用嗎？	How'd it go?	怎麼樣？
Is that all?	沒了嗎？	Want some company?	要人陪嗎？
Not even once?	一次都沒有嗎？	Are you free?	有空嗎？

英文	中譯	英文	中譯
四字問句			
Will you be going?	你會去吧？	Is that so obvious?	有這麼明顯嗎？
Think that's good sign?	你覺得是好徵兆嗎？	When will that be?	到底是什麼時候？
Where have you been?	你去哪裡了？	Was that a coincidence?	那是巧合嗎？
Was that so hard?	這不難吧！	What's so important?	什麼事那麼重要？
Why'd you do that?	你為什麼這麼做？	Who else was there?	還有誰在那裡？
How did you do it?	你是怎麼做到的？	Was there any follow?	有後續報導嗎？
What's on your mind?	你有什麼心事？	Did this just happen?	這是剛發生的事嗎？
Is that long enough?	夠久了吧？	Am I disturbing you?	我有打擾到你嗎？
What was that like?	那是什麼感覺？	You up for this?	你行嗎？
Did you try guessing?	你有試著猜嗎？	What was that about?	那是怎麼回事？
What if he's right?	萬一他說的是真的？	How are we looking?	情況怎麼樣？
Do I sound ready?	我看起來像準備好了嗎？	What is your involvement?	你怎麼參與進來了？
Are we in position?	準備好了嗎？	What do we get?	什麼情況？
Have you googled it?	你上網查了嗎？	You set this up?	你安排的？

英文	中譯	英文	中譯
五字問句			
How do you know that?	你怎麼知道？	What does it look like?	它看起來怎麼樣？
What is this all about?	這是怎麼回事？	Does it sounds that bad?	這聽起來很差勁嗎？
How do you figure that?	為什麼你這麼想？	How long will it last?	會持續多久？
How'd you pull it off?	你是怎麼搞定的？	How long have you known?	你知道多久了？
Not a hard decision, right?	不難決定，是吧？	Why do you do that?	你為何這麼做？
What exactly do you want?	你到底想要什麼？	Have you thought this through?	你真的考慮清楚了嗎？
Did you see what happened?	你知道發生了什麼？	How did you manage it?	你是怎麼辦到的？
What's going to happen here?	接下來會怎樣？	What are you worried about?	你担心什麼？
How's you like that course?	你覺得那堂課如何？	How did this even happen?	這事怎麼會發生？
Did you hear the news?	你看新聞了嗎？	Does that work on people?	那真的管用嗎？
What's in it for you?	到底你有什麼好處？	Why would you do that?	你幹嘛那麼做？
六字問句			
What are we going to do?	我們怎麼辦？	What would you like you know?	你想知道什麼？
What were you guys talking about?	你們談了什麼？	Dose this seem familiar to you?	你們覺得這個熟悉嗎？

英文	中譯	英文	中譯
How are you gonna afford that?	你怎麼負擔得起？	What are you planning to do?	你到底在打什麼主意？
What do you think it means?	你認為那是什麼意思？	Does it make you feel stupid?	這是不是讓你覺得很蠢？
What do I get out of it?	我能得到什麼好處？	How do you want to do?	你想怎麼做？
Does the world care that much?	大家有那麼在乎嗎？	Is that too much to ask?	這要求會太過分了嗎？
What am I getting in return?	我有什麼好處？	What are you doing today?	今天你打算做什麼？

從電影對話中找靈感

▶ Is that American trick?
這就是美國人的詭計嗎？ ………………………………… 🎬 布魯克林

▶ Are you sure this is a good idea?
你確定這是個好主意？ ………………………………… 🎬 我想念我自己

▶ How can you be so cavalier about this?
對這事，你怎麼還能這麼輕鬆呢？ ………………… 🎬 靈犬出任務

▶ How do you get over something like that?
那些狀況你怎麼熬過來的？ ………………………… 🎬 詭影任務

▶ What are you concentrating so hard on?
你這麼專心在做什麼呢？ ………………………………… 🎬 大夢想家

▶ Will you be just straight with me?
你可以跟我說實話嗎？ ………………………………… 🎬 命運鞋奏曲

▶ What happened to make you change your mind?
什麼事讓你改變主意？ ………………………………… 🎬 愛情失控點

▶ Why don't you come and grab a bite with us?
跟我們一起去吃飯吧？ ·· 🎥◀ 拍賣家

▶ I think I'm at least due an explanation.
我認為我至少應有個解釋。 ·· 🎥◀ 拍賣家

▶ How much longer is this gonna take?
這還要多久？ ·· 🎥◀ 跨界失控

▶ Should I be worried about job security?
我應該擔心自己的工作保障嗎？ ···································· 🎥◀ 驚爆焦點

▶ You anticipate more cuts?
你預料有更多的裁員嗎？ ·· 🎥◀ 驚爆焦點

▶ You've put some thought into it. Haven't you?
你是經過深思熟慮的，不是嗎？ ···································· 🎥◀ 與外婆同行

最容易運用的職場關鍵字　Position

　　現今多數汽車都會安裝GPS（Global Positioning System），意思是「全球衛星定位系統」，其中用到position這個字，做為名詞時的意思是「位置；立場；職位；部位」，例如問：「他在那家公司是什麼position（職位）？」在投資領域中，投資持有的股票、債券等商品，也叫做position（部位）。Position做為動詞的意思是「把……放在適當位置；把（產品）打進市場」。

　　Positioning最常用的意思是「定位」，常被用在行銷領域，意思是「確定一個讓你的產品佔據或與眾不同的點，以建立產品在客戶心目中的印象」，例如「可口可樂」帶給客戶的印象是「清涼；歡樂」；「VOLVO」汽車給客戶的印象是「安全」。

　　還有一個容易和positioning混淆的字叫proposition，它的意思是「主張；陳述；論點」，常和value一起使用，例如Customer Value Proposition，縮寫為CVP（客戶價值主張），意思是「一段具有說服力的論點，能清楚地說明公司提供給目標客戶的具體利益」，白話一點就是客戶買你的產品或服務的理由。

Proposition當動詞的意思是「求歡；挑逗」，例如在電影《丹麥女孩》中有句台詞：「He propositioned me.」（他向我調情。）

和position相關的片語有In position，意思是「在適當的位子；在位；就位」，例如在電影中常出現的台詞：「Get in position.」（準備就序。）其他和position相關的用法請參閱以下例句。

1 Position n. 位置

We remained in the 3rd position of operating profits globally.
我們的營業淨利保持在全球第三名的位置。

2 Position n. 立場；態度

What's your position on this problem?
你對這個問題的立場是什麼？

3 Positioning n. 定位

It should be basing on "customer care" upon requests. It is a not a money matter, but it is our positioning.
這應該是根據需求建立在「客戶關懷」的基礎上，這不是錢的問題，而是我們的市場定位。

4 Proposition n. 主張；論點

I am trying to understand what the business proposition is.
我試著想了解這個業務的主張是什麼。

Unit 9　增加互動的簡單對話

　　和老外對話時，有些內容聽不太懂，對方也不會知道，但如果對方說的是問句，他會期待你回答，這時就不能裝傻了，學會一些簡單的回應句子，會非常有用。

簡單回應的語句

英文	中譯	英文	中譯
一字回應			
Barely.	勉強算。	Figures.	就知道。
Mostly.	基本上是。	Ditto.	同上／也一樣。
Humiliating.	真丟人！	Absurd.	荒唐！
Lame.	太差勁了！	Nope.	不是。
二字回應			
Look right.	好像對的。	Barely noticed.	幾乎沒注意到！
Very soon.	非常快。	Always does.	一直都是。
That's hysterical.	這太可笑了。	It's laughable.	太可笑了。
It's everything.	這件事很重要。	It's inappropriate.	很不恰當。
Not currently.	現在沒有。	You'll see.	等著瞧！
It's hilarious.	真有趣。	That's that.	就這麼定了。
Doesn't matter.	沒關係。	Lucky guess.	亂猜的。
That long?	那麼久？	That happens.	這是常事。
This sucks.	這很糟糕。	I'm stunned.	嚇著我了。
I figured.	我估計是。	It's ironic.	真是諷刺。

英文	中譯	英文	中譯
It's iconic.	這是經典。	Super awkward.	超級尷尬的！
Apparently not.	看來不是。	That's unreal.	不像真的。
No worries.	不用客氣。	Can't wait.	等不及了！
Stupid sop.	老套！	That's regret.	有點遺憾！
It's customary.	這是慣例。	It's tricky.	挺棘手的！
三字回應			
That's all right.	沒關係。	Force of habit.	習慣了。
It was sudden.	太突然了。	I've been told.	聽人說過。
Haven't heard him.	沒聽過他。	I thought so.	我就知道。
For a time.	此一時彼一時。	Take my shot.	碰碰運氣。
Not much else.	就這些了。	Maybe a little.	也許有一點。
This is incredible.	真是嘆為觀止！	Something like that.	類似。
I got connections.	我有關係。	Didn't expect this.	真沒想到。
It's not that.	不是那麼回事。	That'd be nice.	可以啊。
I'd love to.	我願意。	That's shame.	太遺憾了！
That's too bad.	太遺憾了！	That's hilarious.	真是好玩！
That's dumb.	那太蠢了。	I'm serious.	我是認真的。
I buy that.	我相信你。	It's a lot.	這很常見。
It still works.	還能用。	As it happens.	碰巧也是。
We better not.	最好不要。	Doesn't mean anything.	不代表什麼。
It's a sign.	這是個預兆。	It's uncanny.	不可思議。
Just fake it.	就瞎掰！	It's dreadful.	太可怕了！
What a shame.	太遺憾了！	It's awfully sudden.	這事太突然。

英文	中譯	英文	中譯
Not like that.	不是那個意思。	I kinda figured.	我也是這麼想。
That sounds right.	聽起來是對的。	This is absurd.	這太荒謬了。
I'm not surprised.	我不感到意外。	Not even close.	算不上。
You never know.	很難說。	That's good guess.	你猜的沒錯。
So save it.	算了吧！	It's an anomaly.	這很反常吧！
四字回應			
It does to me.	對我很重要。	Who gives a shit?	誰在乎呢？
They're worth a lot.	它們值很多錢！	It worth a fortune.	這很值錢。
That's what it's like.	就像這樣。	It's supposed to.	這應該是那樣的。
I will consider it.	我會考慮。	Not even a little.	一點也不像。
It matters to me.	對我很重要。	He's just like me.	他和我一樣。
I'm not impressed.	我不欣賞。	That means a lot.	那很重要。
I wasn't thinking that.	我沒這麼想。	This is just awful.	這很糟糕。
That's not a problem.	這沒什麼。	That's hard to say.	很難說。
I didn't mean to.	我不是故意的。	I don't see it.	我不覺得。
Too soon to say.	現在還很難說。	It worked on me.	對我有效。
That would be awesome.	那就太好了。	Nothing to worry about.	沒什麼好擔心的！
It's a silly habit.	這是個笨習慣。	Hell if I know.	我哪知道。
No more than usual.	和平常差不多。	It's better this way.	這樣最好。

英文	中譯	英文	中譯
五字回應			
I didn't see that coming.	我沒料到會這樣。	It's not what I hear.	我聽說的可不一樣。
It's worse than you think.	比你想像的還糟。	I've been thinking about it.	我倒是想過。
He accidently got it right.	他碰巧猜對了吧！	Those are the exact words.	這就是原話。
That exactly what I want.	那正是我要的。	Probable not gonna be good.	可能不會是好事。
I think you're probably right.	我想你可能是對的。	I can't do this anymore.	我受不了了。
There's nothing we can do.	我們無能為力了。	I kind of like it.	我有點喜歡它。
It really not my business.	真的不關我的事。	It shouldn't be like this.	事情不應該是這樣的。
I wasn't thinking of it.	我還沒想。	It is what it is.	事情就是這樣。
There's a lot to it.	說起來挺複雜的。	It takes a long time.	要很久。
This is a tough break.	真是不走運。	I've heard that before.	我聽人說過。
六字回應			
Do what you want to do.	隨便你吧！	It's a little late for that.	這話為時已晚。
It wasn't as simple as that.	這很難解釋。	What was I supposed to do?	我有什麼辦法？
I guess a sort of does.	我想有一點吧！	This is not a good omen.	這不是好的徵兆。

從電影對話中找靈感

▶ There's always some reason for it.
事出必有因。⋯⋯⋯⋯⋯⋯⋯⋯⋯⋯⋯⋯⋯⋯⋯⋯⋯⋯ 🎥 因為愛你

▶ There's more here that meets the eye.
這裡其實大有文章。⋯⋯⋯⋯⋯⋯⋯⋯⋯⋯⋯ 🎥 時空永恆的愛戀

▶ You don't know the half of it.
有些事你不知道。⋯⋯⋯⋯⋯⋯⋯⋯⋯⋯⋯⋯⋯⋯ 🎥 命運鞋奏曲

▶ It's not unheard of.
又不是什麼稀奇事。⋯⋯⋯⋯⋯⋯⋯⋯⋯⋯⋯⋯⋯⋯ 🎥 心靈大道

▶ I'm not passing that on.
我不會傳達這樣的建議。⋯⋯⋯⋯⋯⋯⋯⋯⋯⋯⋯⋯ 🎥 布魯克林

▶ We have good patter.
我們默契不錯！⋯⋯⋯⋯⋯⋯⋯⋯⋯⋯⋯⋯⋯⋯ 🎥 丹林柯林斯

▶ This isn't how I pictured it.
這和我想像的不一樣。⋯⋯⋯⋯⋯⋯⋯⋯⋯⋯⋯⋯⋯⋯ 🎥 大賣空

▶ There's a nicer way to say that.
何必說得那麼露骨。⋯⋯⋯⋯⋯⋯⋯⋯⋯⋯⋯⋯⋯⋯ 🎥 大賣空

▶ I'm a bit out of my depth.
有點超出我的範圍了。⋯⋯⋯⋯⋯⋯⋯⋯⋯⋯⋯⋯ 🎥 丹林柯林斯

▶ It's not my first language.
這不是我最擅長的。⋯⋯⋯⋯⋯⋯⋯⋯⋯⋯⋯⋯ 🎥 丹林柯林斯

▶ Don't hold your breath.
不要抱太大的期望。⋯⋯⋯⋯⋯⋯⋯⋯⋯⋯⋯⋯ 🎥 我想念我自己

最容易運用的職場關鍵字　**Figure**

同事問你：「Can you check-what are figures in columns E and G?」
（你可以確認一下欄位E和G是什麼數字嗎？）這裡的figure是解釋為
「數字」，但 figure 也可以翻譯成「身材」，例如你看到同事變胖了，可以
提醒說：「You have to watch your figure.」（你得注意身材了。）Figure
做為動詞時意思是「計算；料到」，例如Go figure就是叫別人「好好想一
想」。

和figure相關的片語，最常看到的就是figure out，意思是「料到；
理解；計算出」，例如「I should have figured it out.」（我應該料到的）；
「We got to figure this out.」（我們得想出解決辦法。）其他和 figure 相關
的用法請參閱以下例句。

1 **Figure** n. 數字
My staff will pass out the most recent figures.
我的部屬會把最新數據給大家。

2 **Figure** V. 料到
How do you figure that?
你如何料到的？

3 **Figure out** ph. 理解；明白
I can't figure out why he quit his job.
我無法理解為什麼他要辭掉工作。

Unit 10　對同事評頭論足的對話

　　同事們難免會在一起評論某同事，可能是正面、負面或質疑，這些形容人的英文怎麼說？

從電影對話中找靈感

▶ She's demon.
她是很厲害的角色。……………………………… 🎥 我想念我自己

▶ That's a choosy lady.
好挑剔的女人。………………………………… 🎥 白日夢冒險王

▶ This guy is brilliant.
這傢伙很聰明。………………………………… 🎥 通靈神探

▶ She's really talented.
她很有才華。…………………………………… 🎥 當辣妹來敲門

▶ He's solid.
他可靠。………………………………………… 🎥 丹林柯林斯

▶ He got a good heart.
他心腸非常好。………………………………… 🎥 丹林柯林斯

▶ He's a temperamental guy.
他是性情中人。………………………………… 🎥 史帝夫賈伯斯

▶ Steve is a big-picture guy.
史帝夫是高瞻遠矚的人。……………………… 🎥 史帝夫賈伯斯

▶ He seems like a terrific guy.
他看起來是個很不錯的人。…………………… 🎥 實習大叔

▶ You're sensible.
你很明事理。…………………………………… 🎥 布魯克林

▶ Too observant.
太善於觀察了。 .... 🎥 實習大叔

▶ He is very big hit.
他很討喜。 .... 🎥 布魯克林

▶ He's a bit defensive.
他有點防禦性。 .... 🎥 實習大叔

▶ He's been very generous.
他一直很大方。 .... 🎥 非禮勿弒

▶ She's so judgmental.
她太看不起人了。 .... 🎥 與外婆同行

▶ She's just herself.
她特立獨行。 .... 🎥 安諾瑪麗莎

▶ I gotta say that he got some chops.
我不得不說他有點口才。 .... 🎥 靈犬出任務

▶ Looks like he lost his sense of humor.
看來他失去幽默感了。 .... 🎥 當辣妹來敲門

▶ She always does the unexpected.
她總是出人意表。 .... 🎥 大夢想家

▶ He gets over-passionate about things.
他對於一些事情太熱衷了。 .... 🎥 45 年

▶ You're taking him too seriously.
你把他的話當真。 .... 🎥 白宮風雲

▶ He seems like a smart guy.
感覺他還挺能幹的。 .... 🎥 驚爆焦點

▶ You're a bit of a door-half-open kind of person.
你的性格很容易接受別人。 .... 🎥 非禮勿弒

▶ He must've had a lot of enemies.
他肯定樹敵不少。 .... 🎥 愛情失控點

▶ She doesn't care what people think about her.
她不在意別人對她的看法。 .... 🎥 安諾瑪麗莎

▶ He's kind of character.
他挺難應付的。 ······································· 📹 驚爆焦點

最容易運用的職場關鍵字 | **Sense**

　　當別人表達意見後，若你同意或覺得有理，可以說：「Make sense.」（有道理。）反之，說：「It doesn't make sense.」（這沒有道理。）

　　Sense 做為名詞的意思是「意識；觀念；見識；判斷力」等，例如調侃或批評別人時可以說：「你到底有沒有sense啊？」還有常使用common sense（一般常識）及business sense（商業認知）。Sense 做為動詞的意思是「感覺到；意識到；了解」，例如：「我sense到他今天好像不太開心。」

　　和sense相關的片語，除了make sense，還有in a sense（就某種意義上）。由sense衍生出來的字有nonsense，意思是「胡說；無聊」，講這句話時可以是開玩笑或嚴肅的語氣，端看當時的情境，其他和sense相關的用法請參閱以下例句。

1 **Sense** n. 意識；感知
I got a sense of it already.
我已經感受到了。

2 **Sense** v. 感覺到；意識到
I sensed that I had made a serious mistake.
我意識到自己犯了個嚴重的錯誤。

3 **Make sense** ph. 講得通；有意義；言之有理
You're not making very much sense.
你這說不過去。

4 **In a sense** adj. 在某種意義上
In a sense you are right in refusing to attend the meeting.
在某種意義上，你拒絕參加那個會議是對的。

4 **Nonsense** n. 胡說；胡扯；廢話
You are talking complete nonsense.
你說的全是廢話。

電影經典名言可以這樣應用

銷售主管在訓練業務人員，這句話就可以派上用場，意思就是不要怕失敗，要不斷地嘗試說服客戶。

• A very smart guy once said "You tell somebody something once, they don't listen. You tell somebody four times, they don't listen. By the ninth time you say it, they begin to hear you.
一位智者曾說：「一件事情你和別人講一遍，他不會聽；講四遍了，他們還是不聽，直到講到第九遍時，他們才開始聽到你說的話。
引自《翻轉幸福》

Unit 11　職場各種情境用語

　　除了上述情境外，在職場和同事之間互動，還有各種不同的情境，例如祝賀、感激、訴苦、提醒等，請參閱以下例句。

從電影對話中找靈感

祝賀同事

▶ Got a little surprise for you.
有個驚喜給你。 ………………………………………………………… 🎥 命運鞋奏曲

▶ I just came by to say congratulations.
我是來說恭喜的。 ……………………………………………………… 🎥 白宮風雲

▶ I smell a promotion for you.
我覺得你要升職了。 …………………………………………………… 🎥 非禮勿弒

感激同事

▶ This means so much to me.
這對我意義非凡。 ……………………………………………………… 🎥 翻轉幸福

▶ I still owe you a favor.
我還是欠你一個人情。 ………………………………………………… 🎥 史帝夫賈伯斯

▶ I repay my debts.
我會報答你的。 ………………………………………………………… 🎥 家有兩個爸

▶ Thanks for the warning.
感謝你的警告。 ………………………………………………………… 🎥 搖搖欲墜

▶ We owe you a huge thanks.
我們欠你一個大大的感謝。 …………………………………………… 🎥 加州大地震

▶ That's very kind.
你真客氣。⋯⋯⋯⋯⋯⋯⋯⋯⋯⋯⋯⋯⋯⋯⋯⋯ 🎥◀ 拍賣家

▶ It means a lot to us.
幫了我們大忙。⋯⋯⋯⋯⋯⋯⋯⋯⋯⋯⋯⋯⋯⋯ 🎥◀ 靈犬出任務

向同事訴苦

▶ It's shitting feeling.
感覺很糟糕。⋯⋯⋯⋯⋯⋯⋯⋯⋯⋯⋯⋯⋯⋯⋯ 🎥◀ 驚爆焦點

▶ Tough sit to sit in.
處事不容易啊！⋯⋯⋯⋯⋯⋯⋯⋯⋯⋯⋯⋯⋯⋯ 🎥◀ 驚爆焦點

▶ I just had a stressful afternoon.
我今天下午壓力很大。⋯⋯⋯⋯⋯⋯⋯⋯⋯⋯ 🎥◀ 凸槌三人行

▶ They are kinda of depressing.
會讓我心情低落。⋯⋯⋯⋯⋯⋯⋯⋯⋯⋯⋯⋯ 🎥◀ 驚爆焦點

▶ It makes me uncomfortable.
這讓我不舒服。⋯⋯⋯⋯⋯⋯⋯⋯⋯⋯⋯⋯⋯ 🎥◀ 凸槌三人行

▶ It's just a little annoying.
就是有點煩人。⋯⋯⋯⋯⋯⋯⋯⋯⋯⋯⋯⋯⋯ 🎥◀ 凸槌三人行

▶ It's depressing.
這令人挺鬱悶的。⋯⋯⋯⋯⋯⋯⋯⋯⋯⋯⋯⋯ 🎥◀ 布魯克林

▶ Life is tough.
生活是艱難的！⋯⋯⋯⋯⋯⋯⋯⋯⋯⋯⋯⋯⋯ 🎥◀ 我想念我自己

▶ I'm so sick of it.
我真是受夠了！⋯⋯⋯⋯⋯⋯⋯⋯⋯⋯⋯⋯⋯ 🎥◀ 家有兩個爸

向同事求助

▶ Will you do that for me?
就算是看在我的面子上，可以嗎？⋯⋯⋯⋯ 🎥◀ 史帝夫賈伯斯

▶ You could help grease the wheels a little.
你可以幫忙圓圓場。 ··· 🎥 家有兩個爸

▶ Be more supportive.
多支持一下！ ·· 🎥 跨界失控

▶ Call it a personal favor.
就當是幫我的忙。 ·· 🎥 通靈神探

▶ Next time give me a heads up, okay?
下次先給我透露點風聲，好嗎？ ································· 🎥 驚爆焦點

提醒同事

▶ Just let it go.
放手吧！ ··· 🎥 謎樣的雙眼

▶ You're kind of crossing the line here.
你有點越界了。 ·· 🎥 謎樣的雙眼

▶ Just unsolicited advice.
只是給你一些忠告。 ·· 🎥 謎樣的雙眼

▶ Some things you say, they can be misinterpreted.
你的有些話會被誤解。 ··· 🎥 出棋制勝

▶ Which won't be great in your case.
這對你並不是件好事。 ··· 🎥 實習大叔

▶ I'm just trying to spare you an ass-kicking.
我只是試圖讓你省得被釘。 ·· 🎥 謎樣的雙眼

▶ Keep your eyes peeled.
記得關注！ ··· 🎥 搖搖欲墜

責罵同事

▶ You're full of crap.
少說屁話！ ··· 🎥 白宮風雲

▶ Don't be preposterous.
別胡說八道！ ………………………………………… 🎬 大夢想家

▶ You have a big mouth.
你真是大嘴巴！ ………………………………………… 🎬 驚天換日

▶ How could you do it?
你怎麼做得出啊？ ……………………………………… 🎬 愛情失控點

▶ The arrogance of you.
你太自大了。 …………………………………………… 🎬 心靈大道

▶ It's all to your advantage.
你只顧你的利益。 ……………………………………… 🎬 拍賣家

▶ You stay out of my business.
你少管閒事。 …………………………………………… 🎬 命運鞋奏曲

▶ That's really horrible thing to say.
這話很傷人。 …………………………………………… 🎬 與外婆同行

▶ You don't have to be such a dick.
你不用這麼惹人厭。 …………………………………… 🎬 白日夢冒險王

質疑同事

▶ Don't you think I deserve an explanation?
你不覺得欠我一個解釋嗎？ …………………………… 🎬 愛情沒有終點

▶ That's not going to happen.
這是不可能的事。 ……………………………………… 🎬 實習大叔

▶ Just say something true.
說點實話吧！ …………………………………………… 🎬 紙上城市

▶ You're shitting me?
你沒騙我吧？ …………………………………………… 🎬 驚爆焦點

▶ Are you being sarcastic with us?
你是在挖苦我們嗎？ …………………………………… 🎬 大賣空

▶ I think you're slightly exaggerating.
我覺得你有點誇大了。……………………………… 📹◀ 非禮勿弒

▶ What happened to your self-respect?
你的自尊到哪兒去了？……………………………… 📹◀ 天菜大廚

▶ That's a hard thing to pull off.
這是很難辦到的一件事。…………………………… 📹◀ 實習大叔

▶ It's a little late for that, isn't it?
有點為時已晚了，不是嗎？……………………… 📹◀ 丹林柯林斯

向同事道歉

▶ That was way too far.
說得太過分了。……………………………………… 📹◀ 白宮風雲

▶ I was wrong about you.
我錯怪你了。………………………………………… 📹◀ 空中救援

▶ I'm sorry to put you through it.
抱歉把你拖下水。…………………………………… 📹◀ 全面進化

▶ Sorry, I let you down.
抱歉，我讓你失望。………………………………… 📹◀ 愛情失控點

▶ I owe you an apology.
我欠你一個道歉。…………………………………… 📹◀ 通靈神探

▶ I wanted to tell you I am sorry how I acted yesterday.
我想為我昨天的行為道歉。………………………… 📹◀ 加州大地震

▶ I'm sorry. Obviously, that wasn't a great reaction.
抱歉，顯然那不是該有的反應。…………………… 📹◀ 丹林柯林斯

▶ I'll take an apology for that.
我會為此道歉。……………………………………… 📹◀ 非禮勿弒

▶ I wanted to apologize for earlier.
我想為之前的事道歉。……………………………… 📹◀ 人質

▶ What I said the other day it was totally out of line.
我那天說的話，完全失態了。 ………………………………… 🎥◀ 驚天換日

▶ I feel really so bad I was so sensitive yesterday.
我昨天不應該那麼敏感。 …………………………………… 🎥◀ 我想念我自己

▶ I am sorry I wasn't there this morning.
很抱歉我今天早上沒去。 …………………………………… 🎥◀ 人質

▶ I was a bit of jerk yesterday. I'm sorry about that.
我昨天說話有點過分，抱歉！ …………………………… 🎥◀ 搖滾女王

向同事解釋／求和

▶ Let's let it go now.
我們都放下吧！ …………………………………………… 🎥◀ 史帝夫賈伯斯

▶ You must've misunderstood me.
你肯定是誤解我了。 ……………………………………… 🎥◀ 當辣妹來敲門

▶ I wasn't trying to fool you with this.
我沒想騙你。 ……………………………………………… 🎥◀ 無處可逃

▶ Have I offended you?
我冒犯到你了嗎？ ………………………………………… 🎥◀ 丹麥女孩

▶ Just forget I said anything, okay?
忘了我說的話，好嗎？ …………………………………… 🎥◀ 我想念我自己

▶ I wouldn't do that to you.
我不會對你做這樣的事。 ………………………………… 🎥◀ 我想念我自己

▶ It was just a stupid accident.
就是一個愚蠢的意外。 …………………………………… 🎥◀ 心靈大道

▶ What can I do to make it up to you?
我該怎麼做來補償你？ …………………………………… 🎥◀ 非禮勿弒

▶ Let's clean-slate it.
讓我們重新開始。 ………………………………………… 🎥◀ 實習大叔

▶ Your slate's clean with me.
我們倆就算扯平了。⋯⋯⋯⋯⋯⋯⋯⋯⋯⋯⋯⋯⋯⋯⋯ 🎥 丹林柯林斯

最容易運用的職場關鍵字 **Favor**

　　當你想要求別人幫忙或施予一點恩惠，會用到favor這個字，它可以做為動詞及名詞，主要意思就是「恩惠；善意的行為」，例如在電影《翻轉幸福》中有句台詞說：「I am respectfully asking for the favor that you owe me.」（我向你鄭重提出償還欠我的人情。）和它相關的字有favorite，可以是形容詞或名詞，意思是「最喜歡的人或事」，例如：「Not my favorite.」（不是我最喜歡的。）和favor相關的片語有In favor of（有利於；支持）、do me a favor（幫我個忙），相關用法請參閱以下例句。

---

1 Favor n. 特權
I called in every favor that I knew.
我動用了所有關係。

---

2 Favor n. 偏愛；偏袒
The odds were in my favor.
運氣在我這邊。

---

3 Favorite adj. 喜歡的
Do you have a favorite quote?
你有喜歡的名言嗎？

---

4 In favor of ph. 贊成
To some extent, I'm in favor of your suggestion.
從某種程度上來說，我是贊成你的建議。

---

5 Do me a favor ph. 幫個忙
Could you do me a favor?
能否請你幫我個忙？

解答／十句常用職場應對英文的英譯

1. Let's try not to let it happen again.
2. I'll get on it right away.
3. I want five minutes of his time today.
4. I'll get him. I just need more time.
5. I'm thinking straight.
6. Don't underestimate yourself.
7. You did a good job with your reports.
8. Make this work.
9. Will you be just straight with me?
10. We have good patter.

第 **6** 章

職場中的
電話溝通用語

試試看下列幾句常用的句子，如何用英文表達？

1. 四點半你可以嗎？
2. 我晚點再找你。
3. 你能在二十分鐘內趕到嗎？
4. 他回來後，可以請他打電話給我嗎？
5. 他剛下班。
6. 我試著和安妮連線。
7. 我正在等你電話。
8. 大量購買有折扣嗎？
9. 我幫你轉接給主管。
10. 在我身旁的是南西和賴瑞。

（答案在本章最後一頁）

Unit 1　公司內部的電話應對

　　在大型公司裡，即使是同事也可能分別坐在不同樓層，所以內部電話溝通使用也相當頻繁。有時候寄email給同事，他可能還沒有時間讀若是有時間限制，一般會打個電話提醒一下。

情境模擬對話篇

B Hi Hank. Did you get a chance to look at what I sent you?
嗨，漢克，你有看我寄給你的郵件了嗎？

H Not yet. What was it about?
還沒，是關於什麼？

B It's about the revised proposal of new product.
是關於新產品的修正提案。

H I gotta go to a meeting in just a second. Let's talk later.
我馬上要去開個會，晚點再說！

B Can I meet you this afternoon? 4:30 work for you?
下午我可以見你嗎？四點半你可以嗎？

H Let me check my schedule. Okay, let's shoot for 4:30 p.m.
讓我看看我的時間表。好的，讓我們先敲定下午四點半。

R Is Jessie there?
潔西在嗎？

J Yes, it is. Roy, I've been trying to reach you.
我就是。羅伊，我一直在找你。

R I attended a full-day workshop. That's why it took me so long to call you back.
我參加了一個全天研討會，這就是為什麼這麼久我才回你電話。

J I'm wondering if you'd call me today.
我還在想你今天會不會回我電話。

R Sorry about that.
對不起。

J I sent you an email with a link. Can you take a look?
我寄了一封有連結的郵件給你，你可以看一下嗎？

R Yes, I will. Get back to you tomorrow early morning, okay?
好的，我會的。明天一早回覆妳可以嗎？

J No problem. Thank you for returning my call anyway.
沒問題，無論如何謝謝你回電。

從電影對話中找靈感

▶ I meant to call you.
我正想打電話給你。 .... 📹 45 年

▶ Over here please. Now.
現在請過來一下。 .... 📹 因為愛你

▶ Hold on. I'm on the phone.
稍候，我正在講電話。 .... 📹 白日夢冒險王

▶ I was just about to call you.
我正要打電話給你。 .... 📹 詭影任務

▶ I'll catch up with you later.
我晚點再找你。 .... 📹 實習大叔

▶ Who's on the phone?
誰打的電話？ .... 📹 我想念我自己

▶ I can't figure out how to set up the message box thing.
我不知道怎麼設定語音信箱。 ⋯⋯⋯⋯⋯⋯⋯⋯⋯⋯⋯⋯⋯⋯⋯ 🎥 搖滾女王

最容易運用的職場關鍵字　Call

　　Call最常被解釋為「電話」，例如在規模較大的公司都會設立call center（電話中心），專門受理客戶各種需求。但call也有「請求；招呼」的意思，例如在酒吧中會聽到last call，意思是「最後招呼；最後招待」，也就是最後一輪點餐的機會了。

　　在商用英文中，也常會聽到「It's your call.」，意思是「由你決定；你該決定；你說了算」，但千萬別翻譯成「這是你的電話」，同樣的意思也可以說：「You make the call.」在電影《聖母峰》中有句台詞：「It's his call in the end.」（是他自己決定的。）

　　Call做為動詞時的意思是「打電話；呼喚；召開；稱呼」，例如call a meeting（召開會議），還有「I call him superman.」（我稱呼他「超人」），因為他一天工作16個小時。

　　Call for的意思是「邀請；要求」，例如call for actions（要求行動）。Call back的意思是「收回；回電」，有些公司規定在客戶購買商品後，會有專人負責call back，確定客戶的交易及滿意度。Call off的意思是「取消」，例如取消會議、宴會等，其他和Call相關的用法請參閱以下例句。

1　Call v. 召開

Please call a meeting with relevant stakeholder to close this out.
請與相關的利害相關者召開會議以結束這個（議題）。

2　Call for ph. 要求；需要

June calls for a forecast of $1m but due to the continued market volatility and uncertainties, we are expecting June to be a relatively slow month.
六月份要求的預估值是100萬美元，但由於市場持續波動和不確定性，我們預計六月份會是一個相對清淡的月份。

3 Call back ph. 收回
I think we'd better call back the statement.
我認為我們最好收回聲明。

4 Call off ph. 取消
Mary called off the party due to the terrible weather.
由於天氣惡劣，瑪麗取消了宴會。

換種說法也可通

中譯	常用說法	另類說法
稍候！	Hold on a second.	Hang on a second.《白宮末日》
電話斷線了。	We were disconnected.	I lost him.《家有兩個爸》
打錯號碼了。	Wrong number.	There's been a mistake.《白宮風雲》

電影經典名言可以這樣應用

　　在職場上，這句話可以用在當你想給別人提示時，做為一個引言。

- **A word to the wise here.**
智者一言。　　　　　　　　　　　　　　　　　引自《無處可逃》

Unit 2　緊急來電的應用對話

　　Vincent 和 Judy 外出去廣告公司洽談事情，突然接到老闆祕書 Kelly 的電話，告訴他們老闆 Mike 要召開緊急會議，他們兩人只好取消約會，火速趕回公司。

情境模擬對話篇

K Hi Vincent. It's Kelly.
嗨，文森。我是凱莉。

V Hey, what's up? Is everything alright?
嘿，怎麼了？一切都好嗎？

K Is Judy with you now?
茱蒂現在和你在一起嗎？

V Yes. Speakerphone is what you're on right now.
是的，我開著手機的擴音器呢！

K Where are you?
你們在哪裡？

V We're just on our way to Ogilvy & Mather.
我們剛要去奧美（廣告公司）。

K I know this is short notice. Mike would like to call an urgent meeting at 3:00 p.m.
我知道有點倉促。邁可想在下午三點召開一個緊急會議。

V What happened! Is it serious?
發生什麼事？嚴重嗎？

K Of course. I wouldn't have even bothered to call you. How soon can you come back?
當然，不嚴重的話，我也不會打電話給你們。你們多久可以回來？

V We'll be in the office in 30 minutes.
我們三十分鐘內會到辦公室。

K Good. Talk to you later.
很好，待會兒聊囉！

V See you soon.
待會見！

從電影對話中找靈感

▶ Hey, we're here, so I should really get rolling.
嘿，我們到了，所以我真的得掛電話了。⋯⋯⋯⋯⋯搖搖欲墜

▶ We're headed to the meeting.
我們趕著去開會。⋯⋯⋯⋯⋯⋯凸槌三人行

▶ I'll call you in a bit.
我稍後打給你。⋯⋯⋯⋯⋯⋯⋯凸槌三人行

▶ Can you be over here in 20 minutes?
你能在二十分鐘內趕到嗎？⋯⋯⋯⋯⋯宵禁

▶ Get in your van and get over here.
快上車過來這裡。⋯⋯⋯⋯⋯⋯紙上城市

▶ Sorry I can't come to the phone right now.
抱歉我現在無法接聽電話。⋯⋯⋯⋯⋯人質

▶ That's really why I'm calling you.
這就是我打電話給你的原因。⋯⋯⋯搖滾女王

▶ Can I call you when I get home?
我能回到家再打電話給你嗎？⋯⋯⋯高年級實習生

▶ Be there or be square.
不見不散！⋯⋯⋯⋯⋯⋯⋯⋯實習大叔

▶ I can't seem get a hold of you. Will you please call me at your earliest convenience?

我似乎聯繫不上你，請在你方便的時候盡快回我電話，好嗎？ ⋯⋯⋯⋯⋯

⋯⋯⋯⋯⋯⋯⋯⋯⋯⋯⋯⋯⋯⋯⋯⋯⋯⋯⋯⋯⋯⋯⋯ 🎥 大賣空

最容易運用的職場關鍵字　Speak

　　Speak的意思是「說話；談論；發表演說」，同樣都是「說話」，speak和talk, tell及say 有何不同呢？

　　Speak是用在比較正式的場合，例如：「I can speak French.」（我會說法文。）但和朋友們說話不會用speak，而是用talk，例如：「I talk to my friends.」（我和朋友說話。）Tell的意思是「告訴」，例如：「Tell me the story.」（告訴我這個故事）、「Tell me a secret.」（告訴我一個祕密。）最後還有一個Say（說），一般後面不加受詞，例如：「You know what I'm saying.」（你知道我在說什麼。）

　　Speak up的意思是「大聲說」，在西方文化的職場中，都會特別強調要「Speak up to promote yourself.」（大聲說出來，以推銷自己）。

　　Spoken的意思是「口頭的；口語的」，例如在email的句首常出現Per spoken......（據口頭上說的⋯⋯）。Spokesman的意思是「發言人」，就是公司裡被授權對外及對媒體發言的人，若要特別區分性別，女性便是spokeswoman。

　　Speech的意思是「演講」，做一場演講要用make a speech。在公司的場合中，若某位同事有了好表現，例如業績創新高或得獎，主管在公開場合點名請他上台，下面同事就會鼓噪說：「Speech, speech.」意思就是要他發表感言。其他和speak相關的用法請參閱以下例句。

1 Speak v. 說話；談論；發表演說
Actions speak louder than words.
行動勝於雄辯。

2 Speak of ph. 談到；論及
I am not free on Sundays, not to speak of Mondays.
我星期天都沒空，更不用說星期一了。

---

3 Spoken adj. 口頭講的；口頭的
As spoken, I have added a Gantt chart on slide 6.
如口頭講的，我已經在第六頁加一個甘特圖了。

---

4 Spokesman n. 發言人
This journalist distorted the spokesman's remarks.
這名記者曲解了發言人的話。

電影經典名言可以這樣應用

　　這部電影是描述2008年由美國次級房貸所引發的金融海嘯，當幾位獨具慧眼的天才試圖敲醒那些沉迷於虛幻狂歡的貪婪者時，受到的回應竟是無視和嘲諷，所以影片中出現這段旁白來比喻這種現象。

- **Truth is like poetry. And most people fucking hate poetry.**
  真相就像詩詞，可絕大多數的人都討厭詩詞。　　　引自《大賣空》

Unit 3 代接電話的會話應用

在公司裡幫同事代接電話是常有之事，如何精確說明同事去哪兒（休假、暫時離開座位、外出等），以及留下後續可聯繫的訊息很重要。

情境模擬對話篇

B May I speak to Gary?
可以請蓋瑞聽電話嗎？

A He's just stepped out.
你剛好出去了。

B Do you know when he will be back?
你知道他什麼時候回來嗎？

A I'm not sure. Could be a while.
我不確定，可能要一會兒。

B Will you ask him to call me when he's back?
他回來後，可以請他打電話給我嗎？

A Certainly, your name and phone number, please?
沒問題，請給我你的姓名及電話？

B My name is Andy Fung and the number is 0928000123.
我的名字叫馮安迪，電話號碼是0928000123。

各種「代接電話」的理由

中譯	常用說法	電影來源
他今天休假。	He's not in today.	《驚爆焦點》
他今天休假。	He's taking a personal day.	《凸槌三人行》
她在電話上。	She's on the call.	《實習大叔》
他不在。	He is not available.	《實習大叔》
他今天休假。	He's off today.	X
他現在正在開會。	He's in the meeting right now.	X
他外出了。	He's out.	X
他現在有訪客。	He has visitors right now.	X
他離開座位了。	He is away from his desk now.	X
他休假到下週五。	He is on vacation until next Friday.	X
他剛下班。	He just got off work.	X

最容易運用的職場關鍵字　Step

　　在職場上，常看到有些同事為了求表現，做事不按部就班，喜歡跳過某些步驟，出問題時就會被老闆責罵：「你必須 step by step。」

　　Step 的意思是「步驟；措施；階段；進程」，例如 next step（下個步驟；下個階段）、first step（第一步）、a big step forward（邁進了一大步）。在電影《拍賣家》中有句台詞：「A big step forward, wouldn't you say?」（邁進了一大步，你說對吧？）

　　Step up 的意思是「加快；增加；促進」，例如：「Step up your pace.」（加快速度。）Step by step 的意思是「循序漸進；一步一步來」，例如系統訓練人員帶著我們 step by step 地熟悉系統。其他和 step 相關的用法請參閱以下例句。

1 **Step** n. 步驟；措施；階段；進程
We can have a call to align for next step.
我們可以通個電話，為了下個步驟協調配合。

2 **Step by step** ph. 循序漸進
English can not be learned rapidly; it must be learned step by step.
英語無法快速學會，必須一步步循序漸進地學習。

3 **Step up** ph. 加快；增加；促進
Their social position had been much stepped up.
他們的社會地位已經大大地提高了。

4 **Take steps** ph. 採取措施；採取行動
He knew very well that she had no intention of taking steps.
他非常清楚她不打算採取行動。

電影經典名言可以這樣應用

在開會或討論時，當別人在解釋某事而舉一個例子時，可以用這句話回應，表示已經了解，不必再舉其他例子了。

• **Well you seen one, you seen them all.**
窺一而知全。 引自《時空永恆的愛戀》

Unit 4　與外部交流的電話應對

　　XYZ公司的Jane弄丟了供應商ABC公司的報價單，因為老闆急著想看，她打電話到供應商找不到Annie，於是Annie的同事協助轉接上Annie的手機，幫了Jane的大忙。

情境模擬對話篇

K　ABC company. How can I help you?
ABC 公司，有什麼能幫您的？

J　This is Jane Lu calling from XYZ company. I was trying to reach Annie Wang.
我是盧珍從XYZ公司打來的，我想找王安妮。

K　She is not available right now. Would you like to leave a message?
她現在不在，妳想留言嗎？

J　Any chance you might be able to tell me where she is? It's urgent.
妳可否告訴她在哪裡？我很緊急。

K　Okay, I try to patch Annie through.
好的，我試著和安妮連線。

A　Who's this?
妳是哪位？

K　It's Kelly. I got Jane Lu from XYZ for you.
我是凱莉。XYZ公司的盧安妮在線上。

A Put her through, thanks.
接過來，謝謝！

J Hi, Annie. Am I interrupting anything?
嗨，安妮，我打擾到妳了嗎？

A It's okay. What can I do for you?
沒關係，有什麼能幫妳的？

J I can't find the quotation you sent me before and my boss need it right now. Can you send me again?
我找不到妳之前寄給我的報價單，我老闆現在就要，妳可以再寄給我一次嗎？

A What's your email?
妳的電子郵件是？

J Jane.lu@xyz.com.tw
Jane.lu@xyz.com.tw

A My cell phone number is 0927000123. Don't hesitate to call if you need anything at all.
我的手機號碼是0927000123。有什麼事就馬上聯絡我。

J Thanks a million!
萬分感謝！

從電影對話中找靈感

▶ Get me Senator Russell's office on the phone.
幫我接羅素參議員的辦公室。 ⋯⋯⋯⋯⋯⋯⋯⋯⋯⋯⋯⋯ 🎥 白宮風雲

▶ It's not a good time.
現在不方便。 ⋯⋯⋯⋯⋯⋯⋯⋯⋯⋯⋯⋯⋯⋯⋯⋯⋯⋯⋯⋯ 🎥 白宮末日

▶ Am I disturbing you?
我吵到您了嗎？ ⋯⋯⋯⋯⋯⋯⋯⋯⋯⋯⋯⋯⋯⋯⋯⋯⋯⋯⋯⋯ 🎥 拍賣家

▶ If there's anything else, please don't hesitate to call.
如果還有別的事，請隨時打電話給我。 ⋯⋯⋯⋯⋯⋯⋯⋯⋯ 🎥 拍賣家

▶ Can I come by and see you real quick?
我可以現在過去找你嗎？ ……………………………… 🎬 白宮風雲

▶ Did you just hang up on him?
你剛掛掉他的電話嗎？ ……………………………… 🎬 翻轉幸福

▶ I'll email you the details.
我會把細節發郵件給你。 …………………………… 🎬 愛情沒有終點

▶ I was expecting you to call.
我正在等你電話。 ………………………………………… 🎬 拍賣家

▶ I'll catch you up when I see you.
我們見面再聊吧！ ……………………………… 🎬 白日夢冒險王

▶ I want to meet you to put a face to a name.
我想見你，好把你的臉和名字連在一起。 ………… 🎬 丹麥女孩

▶ I'm so slammed next week.
下周我真忙不過來。 …………………………………… 🎬 實習大叔

▶ I haven't had a lot of time lately.
我最近實在沒時間。 …………………………………… 🎬 驚爆焦點

▶ Let's figure out when we're gonna to meet.
我們商量一下何時見面。 ……………………………… 🎬 翻轉幸福

最容易運用的職場關鍵字 Leave

　　有位金融業的朋友離開原公司，但在短期內卻不能到其他公司上班。因為他正在休 garden leave。這種假並非所有員工都有，一般限於高階主管或特殊職位的員工，原公司要求他們離職後，不能立刻到競爭者的公司上班，中間必須休息幾個月，避免洩漏原公司的最新機密，但代價是在這段休息時間，原公司必須繼續支付薪水。

　　為何稱為 garden leave 呢？這是因為外國人多半住在有前後花園的獨立屋（Detached House），每隔一段時間就得除草及整理花園，而且會花不少時間，因而稱之。

　　Leave 做為名詞的意思是「休假」，上班族有不同的假期，常見的有年假、病假及事假，這些假期的英文該怎麼說，請參閱下表。休假的動詞用 take，也可以直接用 be 動詞，例如：「Emma is on annual leave.」（艾瑪正在休年假。）

英文	中譯	英文	中譯
Personal leave	事假	Sick leave	病假
Leave for statutory reasons	公假	Maternity leave	產假
Paternity leave	陪產假	Parental leave	育嬰假
Marital leave	婚假	Funeral leave	喪假
Leave without pay	留職停薪	Block leave	強制休假（註）

註：外商公司多半都會規定，某個層級以上的員工，一年之中必須休一次超過年假二分之一或十個工作天以上的年假，稱之 block leave。

　　Leave 做為動詞的意思是「離開；把……交給」，例如你告訴老闆或同事：「Leave it to me」（讓我來），其他和 leave 相關的用法請參閱以下例句。

---

1 Leave V. 離開
You may ask staff to leave early today whenever they finish their work.
你可以要求部屬今天提早離開，當他們完成他們的工作。

---

2 Leave V. 把……交給；委託
I leave you to reply.
我留給你回覆。

---

3 Leave n. 休假
Apologize for not reverting earlier as I was on block leave in the past 2 weeks.
很抱歉沒有早一點回覆，因為過去兩週我在休長假。

Unit 5　客戶諮詢產品的電話應對

　　有位客戶主動打電話到總機詢問公司產品，總機將電話轉到業務部門，最後由一位業務代表接聽電話並解決客戶的疑問。

情境模擬對話篇

O ABC company. How may I help you?
ABC 公司，有什麼我可以幫您的？

C I'm interested in your products but I have some questions need to clarify.
我對你們的產品有興趣，但我有一些問題需要澄清。

O Just be one moment. I will find a sales representative for you.
稍候一下。我幫你找一位業務代表。

――――――――――――― 業務部門 ―――――――――――――

A Hey, John. Are you gonna answer that?
嘿，約翰。你要接那個電話嗎？

J I'm afraid I can't. I'm expecting an important customer's call.
我恐怕不行，我正在等一位重要客戶的電話。

A How can I direct the call?
請問電話要轉接給誰？

S Put them through.
接過來。

S Hello, my name is Steven. What should I call you?
哈囉！我是史帝芬。怎麼稱呼您？

C My last name is Yen.
我姓顏。

S Mr. Yen. What can I do for you?
顏先生，有什麼能幫您的？

C I'd like to order some tablets.
我想訂購一些平板電腦。

S How many would you like to order?
您要訂多少？

C One hundred. Do you offer any quantity discounts?
一百台。大量購買有折扣嗎？

S Yes, we can offer a 10% discount for orders over 100.
有的，訂購一百台以上，我們可以打九折。

C Great. I 'll give you a call when we are ready to order.
太好了，等我們準備好訂購時，我會打電話給你。

S May I leave your contact information?
我可以留一下你的聯絡訊息嗎？

C Sure. My office number is 02-87813888.
當然。我辦公室電話號碼是02-87813888。

從電影對話中找靈感

▶ Can I borrow pencil and paper?
能借一下紙和筆嗎？ ·· 🎥 因為愛你

▶ Please hold.
請不要掛斷。 ·· 🎥 凸槌三人行

▶ We lost the connection.
斷線了。 ·· 🎥 凸槌三人行

▶ There's a call for you on Line One.
一號線有你的電話。 ······································· 🎥 史帝夫賈伯斯

▶ Hold on, let me get you the hotline number.
等一下，我給你熱線號碼。 ⋯⋯⋯⋯⋯⋯⋯⋯⋯⋯⋯⋯⋯⋯ 📹 人質

▶ How long will it arrive?
多久才會送到呢？ ⋯⋯⋯⋯⋯⋯⋯⋯⋯⋯⋯⋯⋯⋯⋯⋯ 📹 因為愛你

▶ Sorry, I didn't get what you said.
對不起，我沒聽懂你說的話。 ⋯⋯⋯⋯⋯⋯⋯⋯⋯⋯⋯ 📹 白宮風雲

▶ Would you say that again?
你能再說一遍嗎？ ⋯⋯⋯⋯⋯⋯⋯⋯⋯⋯⋯⋯⋯⋯⋯⋯ 📹 白宮風雲

▶ Please speak a little louder.
請講大聲一點。 ⋯⋯⋯⋯⋯⋯⋯⋯⋯⋯⋯⋯⋯⋯⋯⋯⋯ 📹 白宮風雲

最容易運用的職場關鍵字　Clarify／Verify

　　Clarify和verify這兩個字的拼法及發音都有點相似，有時容易造成混淆而使用錯誤。Clarify的意思是「澄清；闡明」，例如某件事情說明的不清楚，就會要求對方：「Please help clarify.」（請幫忙澄清。）

　　而 verify 的意思是「證明；證實」，就是要證實某件事的正確性或真實性，例如這件事需要再verify，另外有些行業在交易時需要先verify客戶的印鑑或簽名。

　　Clarify和verify的名詞，分別為clarification及verification，意思和動詞相同。任何系統的上線，都必須經過一道關卡，稱為UVT（User Verification Test），其中的V就是verification，實務上會找使用者輸入真實資料，進行測試系統是否正常。相關用法請參閱以下例句。

1 Clarify Ⓥ 澄清；闡明
Feel free to contact me if you need any clarification.
請隨時與我聯繫，如果您需要任何澄清。

2 Clarification n. 澄清；闡明
I hope this email is able to clarify the situation.
我希望這封電子郵件是能夠澄清這個狀況。

3 Verify v. 證明；證實
It was easy to verify his statements.
他的話很容易證實。

4 Verification n. 證明；證實
I think signature verification should be done independently in a different platform.
我認為驗證簽名應該在不同的平台上獨立完成。

電影經典名言可以這樣應用

　　這句話適用在你拜訪別的公司或別的國家時，同意遵照別人的習慣或習俗時。

• **When in Rome!**
入境隨俗！

引自《大夢想家》

<table>
<tr><td>Unit
6</td><td>客訴服務的電話應對</td></tr>
</table>

　　有位客戶在兩周前買了一台果汁機，前兩天才發現無法正常使用，想拿到店裡去更換，店員因公司要求七天內才能退還的政策而拒絕他，於是客戶打電話到總公司的電話客服中心客訴，要求更換新的果汁機或退費。

情境模擬對話篇

O Thank you for calling ABC company. How may I help you?
謝謝致電ABC公司，有什麼我可以幫您的？

A I would like to make a complaint about a blender I bought from your company recently.
我想提出投訴，關於最近我在你們公司購買的果汁機。

O Could you tell me the details?
可以告訴我細節嗎？

A The blender does not work properly. And I requested to replace a new one and was rejected by your salesperson at store.
果汁機不能正常使用。我要求更換一個新的，但被你們店裡的銷售人員拒絕了。

O How long have you bought?
你買多久了？

A Two weeks. But I just started to use it recently.
兩周。但是我最近才開始使用。

O According to our return policy, if you wish to return it, you have a period of 7 days from the date of purchase to return.
根據我們的退貨政策，如果你想退貨，你必須在購買日起的7天內退還。

A Can I speak to your supervisor or someone else who can help me?
我要和你的主管或其他可以幫我處理的人通話？

O Please hold....... Thank for you holding. I'll patch you through my supervisor.
請稍待……感謝等候。我幫你轉接給主管。

持續抱怨

A I would like to resolve this between us. If we can't, I will refer it to Consumers' Foundation.
我想在我們之間解決這個問題。如果不能，我會把它轉到消基會。

M No worry. Let me fix that for you.
不用擔心，讓我來幫您處理。

A Thanks for your help. I look forward to hearing from you in the next 5 days.
感謝你的幫助，我期待著在接下來的5天內，得到您的回應。

M Have a nice day. Goodbye.
祝您有美好的一天！再見。

從電影對話中找靈感

▶ Please hold. Your call is very important to us.
請稍候，我們非常重視您的來電。…………………… 🎥 因為愛你

▶ I'm filing a complaint.
我要正式投訴。 ··· 奮鬥的喬伊

▶ My system is down. I need to speak with a technician.
我的系統掛了，我需要和一位技術人員說話。 ·················· 白宮風雲

▶ Sorry for the inconvenience madam.
女士，很抱歉造成不便。 ····································· 因為愛你

▶ For verification purposes, can I get your cellphone number and birthdate?
為了驗證的目的，我可以要您的手機號碼和生日嗎？ ········ 心靈大道

▶ May I please get your account number and the name on the account?
我可以要您的帳號和帳戶上的名字嗎？ ···················· 心靈大道

▶ How long will it take?
需要多長的時間？ ·· 白宮風雲

▶ The whole process usually just takes 2-3 days.
整個流程通常只需要二到三天。 ····························· 白宮風雲

▶ Would that be alright?
那樣可以嗎？ ·· 白宮風雲

▶ Is there anything else that I could assist you with?
還有什麼我可以幫您的嗎？ ································· 因為愛你

▶ You have a great day and thanks for calling.
祝您有個愉快的一天，謝謝來電！ ··························· 因為愛你

最容易運用的職場關鍵字 | Hold

　　講電話時要對方稍候，可以說：「Hold on, please.」（請不要掛電話。）在商用英文中，Hold 常解釋為「認為；持有」，例如：「She holds the same view.」（她持有相同的看法。）

　　例如九月底有一筆收入匯進來，你問主管要不要在九月入帳，主管看了一下九月業績已達標，便說：「Hold to October.」，意思是留到十月再入帳，此時的 hold 解釋成「握住；抓住」。

　　和 Hold 相關的片語，除了常用的 hold on（停下來；保持）外，還有 hold back（保留；阻止）及 on hold（擱置；凍結），例如在電影《翻轉幸福》中有句台詞：「Maybe your dreams are on hold right now.」（也許你的夢想只是暫時擱置一下而已。）

　　由 hold 所衍生出來的字有 stakeholder（利害相關者）、uphold（支持；贊成）、holder（持有人）、holding（持有物）、holdingcompany（控股公司）。Stakeholder 是指和某件事情有利害相關的部門及同事，其他與 hold 相關的用法請參閱以下例句。

---

1 Hold v. 舉行；舉辦
They will hold a meeting to discuss this subject tomorrow.
他們明天將開會討論這個議題。

---

2 On hold ph. 擱置；凍結
All regulatory approvals are currently on hold.
所有主管機關的核准現在都是擱置。

---

3 Uphold v. 支持；贊成
I believe we need to uphold a single pricing strategy that offer products across many countries.
我相信我們需要支持單一定價策略以在許多國家提供產品。

---

4 Holding company n. 控股公司
Julie is the CFO（Chief Finance Officer）of XYZ holding company.
茱莉是 XYZ 控股公司的財務長。

Unit 7　電話會議的對話應用

電話會議的運用，讓分布在各國的工作者可以隨時討論重要事項

情境模擬對話篇

K　Hi Stella. This is Kevin from Taiwan. I'm calling in with Cathy and Terry.
嗨，史特拉，我是台灣的凱文，和我參加電話會議還有凱西和泰瑞。

C&T　Hello, Stella.
哈囉，史特拉。

S　Hi guys. Just a moment. We're waiting for Hong Kong team dialing in.
嗨，大家好，稍等一下。我們正在等待香港團隊撥進來。

V　Hello, is anybody there?
哈囉，有人在嗎？

S　Is Vicky? We are already here. Is anybody with you?
維琪嗎？我們都在了，有人和妳一起參加嗎？

V　Yes. I'm here with Nancy and Larry.
有，在我身旁的是南西和賴瑞。

S　Great. We are all here. Today we're talking about our new product approval procedure. I'm sure you have some questions and feedback on it. Let's get started with our COO（Chief Operating Officer）, Steve. He's been working on the procedure for the past month. Steve, what can you tell us why we need a new one?
太好了！所有人都到齊了。今天，我們要談論我們的新產品核准程

序。我敢肯定你們一定有些問題和回饋。我們先從首席運營長史帝夫先開始吧！過去一個月他一直在做這個程序。史蒂夫，你能告訴我們為什麼我們需要有一個新程序？

說明溝通

S Thanks, Steve. The next speaker on our agenda is from our Risk Management department. James, tell us what the requirements from you.
謝謝史帝夫。議程上的下一位發言者是從風險管理部門來的詹姆斯。詹姆斯，告訴我們你們的要求。

討論

V James, can you hold off on that for just a minute? Larry would like to highlight an issue.
詹姆斯，你可以暫停一下嗎？賴瑞想強調一個議題。

S Larry, that's a valid point, but let's take it offline after the meeting.
賴瑞，這是個令人信服的觀點，但是，讓我們等會議結束後再討論。

S Alright, nice call everyone. We decided to rewrite the procedure, so Steve, please get started on that ASAP.
好的，很好的電話會議。我們決定重寫程序，所以史蒂夫請盡快開始修改。

S We'll meet again when the procedure gets finalized. Thank you guys. Talk to you soon.
當程序確認後，我們會再開會。謝謝大家，很快再聊！

從電影對話中找靈感

▶ Speak up! I can't really hear you.
大聲點！我聽不大清楚。⋯⋯⋯⋯⋯⋯⋯⋯⋯⋯⋯⋯⋯ 🎬 布魯克林

▶ London, you still on the conference call?
倫敦的同事們，你們還在電話會議上嗎？ ·················🎬 家有兩個爸

▶ It's Charlie. I'm here, too.
我是查理，我也在這邊。 ·················🎬 大賣空

▶ Ben, you still there?
班，你還在嗎？ ·················🎬 大賣空

▶ Can you hang on a second?
你可以稍等一下嗎？ ·················🎬 白日夢冒險王

▶ I'm sitting here with someone who would like to say hello to you.
我和某個人坐在一起，他想跟你打招呼。 ·················🎬 白宮末日

▶ It was nice to finally talk with you.
很高興終於能和你說上話。 ·················🎬 愛情沒有終點

▶ I hardly got cell phone and Wi-Fi service.
我這裡行動電話及無線網路的訊號都不好。 ·················🎬 大賣空

▶ I'm glad to hear your voice.
很高興聽到你的聲音。 ·················🎬 安諾瑪麗莎

▶ I've been trying you for two hours.
我已經呼叫你兩個小時了。 ·················🎬 凸槌三人行

最容易運用的職場關鍵字 **Line**

聽到line這個字，就會想到手機通訊應用程式LINE，在能連接網路的情況下，可以隨時隨地享受免費簡訊及通話。在電腦網路領域裡，online及offline的意思就是連線及離線，例如online game（線上遊戲），還有一個名詞叫O2O（Online to Offline），意思是將消費者從網路上帶到實體商店，例如網路團購折價券就是一種O2O。

Online及offline還有其衍生之意，在一般會議中討論稱為online，但若某個議題不涉及與會的人或不適合在會議中討論，就會說：「Can we take it offine?」（我們可以會後再談嗎？）

在公司報告系統（reporting line）中，可分為solid line及dot line，前者是指你的直屬主管（line manager），也就是決定考績、升遷及加薪的人，而後者是虛線報告，有些職位還需要報告給區域主管或相關部門的主管，而且在打考績時，直屬主管也會詢問他們的意見。

在行銷領域中，有所謂的above the line（ATL）及below the line（BTL），它是兩種和消費者溝通、建立公司形象的不同行銷手法。ATL會利用媒體，例如電視、報紙、雜誌等，將產品或服務的訊息釋放給不特定的大眾；BTL則是利用一些廣告文宣 DM，鎖定特定的銷售族群，兩者各有其優缺點，多半會一起搭配使用，形成一套完整的行銷策略。

由line所衍生出來的字還不少，包括 deadline（期限）、headline（頭條新聞）、hotline（熱線電話）、bottom line（底線）及pipeline（表示進行中的；正在開發的新產品），其他和line相關的用法請參閱以下例句。

1 Bottom line n. 底線

The bottom line we are expecting in Q1 will be NT$20mn for sales.

我們期待第一季銷售量的底線是新台幣2,000萬元。

2 Guideline n. 指導方針

The enclosed document is a guideline on using the MIS（Management Information System）and how to monitor your sales activities.

所附文件是使用資訊管理系統和如何監督銷售活動的指導方針。

3 Outline n. 大綱

Please prepare and brief an outline of what you would like to discuss at the offsite.

請準備及簡述你想在公司外的會議所討論的大綱。

4 In line with ph. 符合；與……一致

His views are exactly in line with mine.

他的觀點和我完全一致。

Unit 8　社交網路的溝通對話

　　隨著網路科技發達，現代人的溝通方式，已從電話轉變為Twitter、Facebook、Instagram、Facetime、Line及WeChat等社交通訊工具。

情境模擬對話篇

B Mitch, are you there?
米契你在嗎？

螢幕顯示已讀

B Why aren't you answering me?
你怎麼不回我？

A Can we Facetime that?
我們可以在視頻裡聊嗎？

B Okay.
好的。

改為視頻

B I can't hear you.
我聽不到。

A Turn up the volumn.
調大音量啊！

B Oh, it's muted. Sorry!
喔，現在是靜音。抱歉！

A Can you hear me now?
現在聽得到了嗎？

B Loud and clear.
聽得非常清楚。

A Where r u?
你在哪裡？

B I'm on the way home.
我在回家的路上。

A I got something to show you. Just a minute.
我給你看個東西。等一下！

B Delivered.
已傳送。

A Like it won't click.
好像點不了。

B You froze.
你定格了！

A Ugh! Dead zone.
可惡！完全沒訊號了。

從電影對話中找靈感

▶ Let me Instagram this.
讓我拍張照上傳Instagram。 ················ 高年級實習生

▶ Turn the network back on.
重開網路。 ················ 空中救援

▶ Shoot me a text sometime.
偶爾傳簡訊給我。 ················ 高年級實習生

▶ It's one of the most popular apps in the world.
那是全球最受歡迎的應用程式之一。 ················ 實習大叔

▶ It's just probably a glitch.
可能就是小故障而已。 ················ 弒訊

▶ Try to find the IP address.
試著找出IP位址。⋯⋯⋯⋯⋯⋯⋯⋯⋯⋯⋯⋯⋯⋯⋯⋯ 🎬 弒訊

▶ I did notice that your status popped up to single.
我看到你的個人狀態更新為單身了。⋯⋯⋯⋯⋯⋯ 🎬 我想念我自己

▶ I sent you the Facebook page a long time ago.
很久之前我寄給你過我的臉書網頁。⋯⋯⋯⋯⋯⋯ 🎬 搖滾女王

▶ He also makes copious use of the smiley face emoji.
他還發了很多笑臉符號的圖案。⋯⋯⋯⋯⋯⋯⋯⋯ 🎬 搖滾女王

▶ I will tweet this to you.
我會推特這個給你。⋯⋯⋯⋯⋯⋯⋯⋯⋯⋯⋯⋯⋯⋯ 🎬 丹林柯林斯

▶ You want to Netflix something?
你想在Netflix上播些什麼來看嗎？⋯⋯⋯⋯⋯⋯⋯ 🎬 高年級實習生

▶ The blog doesn't do it justice.
比部落格上面介紹得還好。⋯⋯⋯⋯⋯⋯⋯⋯⋯⋯⋯ 🎬 丹林柯林斯

最容易運用的職場關鍵字　Turn

　　有次香港同事來台灣旅遊，我帶他出去吃飯，結帳時兩個人搶著付帳，我就說：「This is my treat.」（我來付帳。）同事知道我很堅持後就說：「OK, but my turn next time.」（好吧，但下次換我請。）此時的turn做為名詞，意思是「依次輪流時各自的一次機會」。

　　Turn也常解釋為「轉動；轉向；轉成」，例如坐計程車時告訴司機：「Make a right turn, please.」（請右轉。）還有，工作若進行到將出現較大成效時可以說：「We're at a turning point.」（我們來到轉捩點了。）

　　和turn相關的片語，常用的有turn on（打開；發動；取決於）、turn off（關掉；解雇）、turn up（開大）、turn into（變成）、turn down（拒絕）、turn out（在場；出席）及turn over a new leaf（展開新的一頁）等。

　　由turn所衍生出的字有turnover，它可以解釋為股票市場的「成交量」、公司的「營業額」、公司人員的「流動率」。還有turnaround（周

轉時間；好轉），商用英文中常見的縮寫TAT，意指turnaround time，表示要完成一件事，來回需要的時間。其他和turn相關的用法請參閱以下例句。

1 **Turn** v. 轉成
YTD（Year to Date）profit & loss has turned positive for the first time.
年初至今的損益第一次轉為正數。

2 **Turn down** ph. 拒絕
Jerry finally turned down the offer letter.
傑瑞最終拒絕了這個工作（錄用通知）。

3 **Turn out** ph. 證明是；結果是
It turned out that my worries were justified.
事實證明，我的擔心不是多餘的。

4 **Turnover** n. 周轉率
Why does your department have such a high turnover rate?
你們部門人員的周轉率為什麼這麼高呢？

5 **Turnaround** n. 轉好
He has passed the most difficult period and could see a turnaround this year.
他已度過最艱難時期，能預見今年情況將會好轉。

電影經典名言可以這樣應用

這句話可以用在鼓勵別人向前看，忘了過去，尤其是負面的陰影。

- **It's really important to not look back.**
  不再回首過去真的很重要。

引自《非禮勿弒》

解答／十句常用電話英文的英譯

1. 4:30 work for you?
2. I'll catch up with you later.
3. Can you be over here in 20 minutes?
4. Will you ask him to call me when he's back?
5. He just got off work.
6. I try to patch Annie through.
7. I was expecting you to call.
8. Do you offer any quantity discounts?
9. I'll patch you through my supervisor.
10. I'm here with Nancy and Larry.

附錄 電影中英文片名對照

英文片名	台灣片名	作者評級
45 Years	45 年	★★★
Captive	人質	★★★
Saving Mr. Banks	大夢想家	★★★★
The Big Short	大賣空	★★★★
Danny Collins	丹林科林斯	★★★★★
The Danish Girl	丹麥女孩	★★★★
Good Will Hunting	心靈捕手	★★★★★
Pawn Sacrifice	出棋制勝	★★
San Andreas	加州大地震	★★★
Carol	因為愛你	★★★★
Steve Jobs	史帝夫賈伯斯	★★★
Anomalisa	安諾瑪麗莎	★★★
Brooklyn	布魯克林	★★★★
The Secret Life of Walter Mitty	白日夢冒險王	★★★★
White House Down	白宮末日	★★★★
The West Wing	白宮風雲	★★★
Oddball	靈犬出任務	★★★★
Transcendence	全面進化	★★★
Project Almanac	跨界失控	★★★
Daddy's Home	家有兩個爸	★★★
Still Alice	我想念我自己	★★★★★
The best offer	拍賣家	★★★
Boulevard	心靈大道	★★★
Non-Stop	空中救援	★★★★
Silver Linings Playbook	派特的幸福劇本	★★★★★

英文片名	台灣片名	作者評級
The Gift	非禮勿弒	★★★
Curfew	宵禁	★★★
The Age of Adaline	時空永恆的愛戀	★★★★
Paper Towns	紙上城市	★★★
The Intern	高年級實習生	★★★★★
The Book Thief	偷書賊	★★★★★
Unfinished Business	凸槌三人行	★★★★
Solace	通靈神探	★★★
The Longest Ride	愛情沒有終點	★★★★
Irrational Man	無理之人	★★★★
No Escape	無處可逃	★★★★
Man on a Ledge	驚天換日	★★★★
Everest	聖母峰	★★★
Tumbledown	搖搖欲墜	★★★
Ricki and the Flash	搖滾女王	★★★★
Unfriended	弒訊	★★
Jack Ryan: Shadow Recruit	傑克萊恩：詭影任務	★★★★
The Internship	實習大叔	★★★★
Knock-knock	當辣妹來敲門	★★
Grandma	與外婆同行	★★★★
The Cobbler	命運鞋奏曲	★★★★
Joy	翻轉幸福	★★★★★
Ex Machina	機械姬	★★
Burnt	天菜大廚	★★★
The Secret in their Eyes	謎樣的雙眼	★★★★
Spotlight	驚爆焦點	★★★★★
Sleeping with Other People	愛睡在一起	★★★

國家圖書館出版品預行編目（CIP）資料

每周一部電影，增進職場英文力／楊偉凱著.
— 初版. — 臺北市：商周出版：家庭傳媒城邦
分公司發行, 民105.10
　　面；　　公分 —（新商業周刊叢書；606）
ISBN 978-986-477-104-2（平裝）

1.英語　2.職場　3.讀本

805.18　　　　　　　　　　　　105016836

新商業周刊叢書 619

每周一部電影，
增進職場英文力

作　　　者／楊偉凱
責 任 編 輯／張曉蕊
版　　　權／黃淑敏
行 銷 業 務／莊英傑、石一志、周佑潔

總 編　輯／陳美靜
總 經　理／彭之琬
發 行　人／何飛鵬
法 律 顧 問／台英國際商務法律事務所
出　　　版／商周出版
　　　　　　台北市中山區民生東路二段141號4樓
　　　　　　電話：（02）2500-7008　　傳真：（02）2500-7759
　　　　　　E-mail：bwp.service@cite.com.tw
發　　　行／英屬蓋曼群島商家庭傳媒股份有限公司　城邦分公司
　　　　　　台北市中山區民生東路二段141號2樓
　　　　　　電話：（02）2500-0888　　傳真：（02）2500-1938
　　　　　　讀者服務專線：0800-020-299　　24小時傳真服務：（02）2517-0999
　　　　　　讀者服務信箱：service@readingclub.com.tw
　　　　　　郵撥帳號：19833503
　　　　　　戶名：英屬蓋曼群島商家庭傳媒股份有限公司　城邦分公司
香港發行所／城邦（香港）出版集團有限公司
　　　　　　香港灣仔駱克道193號東超商業中心1樓
　　　　　　電話：（852）2508-6231　　傳真：（852）2578-9337
　　　　　　E-mail：hkcite@biznetvigator.com
馬新發行所／城邦（馬新）出版集團
　　　　　　【Cite (M) Sdn.Bhd. (458372U)】
　　　　　　11, Jalan 30D/146, Desa Tasik, Sungai Besi,
　　　　　　57000 Kuala Lumpur, Malaysia
　　　　　　電話：（603）9056-3833　　傳真：（603）9056-2833

封 面 設 計／黃聖文
內 文 製 作／黃淑華
印　　　刷／鴻霖印刷傳媒有限公司
總 經　銷／聯合發行股份有限公司
　　　　　　電話：（02）2917-8022　　傳真：（02）2915-6275